WICKED WAYS

WICKED WAYS

DONNA HILL

ST. MARTIN'S PRESS
NEW YORK

This is a work of fiction. All of the characters, organizations, and events portrayed in this novel are either products of the author's imagination or are used fictitiously.

www.stmartins.com

Design by Maggie Goodman

Library of Congress Cataloging-in-Publication Data

Hill, Donna (Donna O.)
    Wicked ways / Donna Hill.—1st ed.
        p.   cm.
    ISBN-13: 978-0-312-35422-0
    ISBN-10: 0-312-35422-3
    1. Women murderers—Fiction.   2. Escort services—Fiction.   3. Aruba—Fiction.
I. Title.

PS3558.I3864H55   2007
813'.54—dc22

                                                              2007022460

First Edition: October 2007

10   9   8   7   6   5   4   3   2   1

Wicked Ways *is dedicated to all my crazy fans,*
supportive book clubs, folks on the street, and the
friends and family who threatened to kick me to the
literary curb if I didn't hurry up with this sequel.
Thanks so much for wanting me to do what I love.
So here it is, hope ya'll enjoy it!

acknowledgments

WRITING IS SUCH a solitary profession, but what makes it all worthwhile are the folks in your life that cheer you on and inspire you. I want to send out my sincere thanks and gratitude to my fellow authors who inspire me through their work: my dear friends Gwynne Forster, L. A. Banks, Rochelle Alers, Francis Ray, Bernice McFadden, Lolita Files, Victoria Christopher Murray; bookclub diva Tee Royal; my sisterfriends Missy Brown, Pittershawn Palmer, Deb Owsley, Linda Walters, Jessica McClean, and Peggy Hicks; brotherfriends Vincent Alexandria, Victor McGlothin, and William Frederick Cooper; Nathasha Brooks-Harris, who gave me my start; my divine sister in spirit, Antoinette Hutchinson; my sister and best friend Lisa Hill, my mom, who still believes I'm wonderful, my brother David and my brood Nichole, Dawne, Matthew, Mahlik, and Makayla. Of course I could be doing all this writing and not have anywhere to show it off, so big thanks go out to my wonderful editor, Monique Patterson, the St. Martins family, and the best agent in the universe, Pattie Steele Perkins. But when it is all said and done, nothing is possible without God, who has bestowed upon me a wonderful gift, and I promise to continue to use it wisely and to my best ability.

WICKED WAYS

KILLING VINCENT WASN'T PART of her plan. He should have stayed in New York and left well enough alone. He shouldn't have contacted her—told her that he knew everything—told her that he would not allow her to continue hurting people.

Vincent. Damn you.

Tess McDonald's pulse beat a little faster. She'd been in love with Vincent, and if she really thought about it, she still was, at least as much as she allowed herself to love anyone. That made what she had to do so much more difficult. However, she didn't live in the kind of world where love was an option. Allowing feelings to enter into her life resulted in this—a rendezvous with murder.

Tess eased her rented white sports car along the dark narrow roads. A light drizzle fell onto the windshield. The full moon's iridescent light flashed from behind the tops of swaying palm trees.

She'd come to Aruba not only to recover from months of tension, anxiety, and murders, but also to reestablish her business. For more than a decade she'd been the highest paid and most influential madam on the East Coast.

A rueful smile tugged the corners of her full mouth. She'd worked hard to assemble her elite stable of women and develop her powerhouse clientele list. She'd had a multimillion-dollar business, and Tess intended to reclaim it here in Aruba. Her former clients included everyone from Fortune 500 CEOs to politicians and judges. The key to her long-standing success was discretion, for which she'd been well compensated.

Life had been good—until Tracy got too close. That her own sister had been the catalyst for the demise of her business was unfortunate, to say the least. Tracy's zeal as an assistant district attorney for New York City—always on the side of justice, law, and order—led directly to her death. Life was full of ironic twists, wasn't it?

Tess would never forget the night of the newscast that detailed the gunning down of Assistant DA Tracy Alexander. Her sister. Dead.

Now Tess was once again on the precipice of loss. It's always those closest to you that brought the most harm, she mused, navigating the gravel road. Perhaps she didn't keep her enemies close enough. She almost laughed. Almost.

After relocating to Aruba it had taken her months to get set up again: to recruit the perfect women, to cultivate relationships with the men of wealth who lived on the island, as well as with those who visited on holiday. Tonight's elaborate gathering at her secluded villa was the culmination of all her work. She'd left her guests in the capable hands of Charrie Lewis. Hopefully, this task wouldn't take long and she'd be able to return before she was truly missed.

She'd gotten Charrie, her original business partner from back in the city, to join her. Tess trusted Charrie implicitly. Equally important, she'd convinced Nicole and Kim that if they joined her as well, they could finally be free from their pasts. They would reap the rewards that were due them. But then Vincent had found her. Tracked her all the way here from New York.

She couldn't let him ruin it all—and not just for her sake but for that of everyone else she'd enlisted. Nicole and Kim had risked everything, committing crimes from which they'd ultimately walked away scot-free, crimes she'd convinced them to commit. The three of them were bound by that secret. It was up to her to ensure that their pact was never discovered. Only Vincent stood between them and total freedom.

The skyline lit up with electricity and thunder exploded overhead. Adrenaline surged through her veins.

She pulled up to the motel where she was to meet Vincent, and slowed the car. Her .38 was tucked neatly inside her purse on the passenger seat. What did Vincent have planned for her? Would he make a scene? Were the local police waiting?

No. Vincent would do this alone. She knew him. He loved his autonomy. Yes, it would be just the two of them, face-to-face.

VINCENT STEPPED OUTSIDE, looked skyward. A storm was brewing. It was close. A light sprinkle danced around him.

He lit a cigarette and blew a plume of smoke into the muggy air. The fleeting scent of sulfur wafted beneath his nose.

He peered into the darkness, the moon obscured now by thick-ening clouds. Tess was close. He could feel her as surely as he could feel the bulging erection pressing against the fabric of his jeans. An-ticipation of a bust always did that to him, and so did Tess McDon-ald. He'd let that personal flaw cloud his objectives once. Not again.

Headlights drew closer and then stopped. A car door opened. Vincent reached for his gun.

Thunder boomed. Vincent felt a searing pain in his side. His legs gave out. His .45 slipped from his hands to the sandy ground. He followed suit.

Tess pressed her body against a tree, standing stock still. Her heart was pounding so violently, her head began to throb. She lis-tened for sound—for movement. When she was sure it was safe to do so, she stepped out into the moonlight. The shape of a sprawled body was ahead. Crouching and with her gun at the ready, she ran over to the motionless form.

Blood pooled beneath him. Tess listened intently for any hint that the gunshot had been heard by the local residents or passersby. She grabbed the limp body beneath its damp armpits and dragged the dead weight to her car.

Vincent groaned. Blood flowed onto the soft leather seat. Tess stepped on the gas. *Not too fast,* she cautioned herself. The last thing she needed was to draw attention to herself by speeding.

Suddenly the sky opened up, and the deluge nearly blinded her. Within moments the wipers were useless. Tess gripped the steering wheel, trying in vain to see the road ahead. She stole a glance at her wounded passenger. Sweat drenched his forehead.

Shit!

Headlights appeared in her rearview mirror. Her heart pumped faster. Should she speed up or slow down?

The other car's horn honked. The driver had switched on the turn signal. Tess eased her car to the right side of the road, and the other car sped up and went around her.

Tess released the breath that had lodged in the center of her chest. Vincent groaned again.

She had to find sanctuary, and she had to get rid of the car. There was only one place she could go.

He may be a man of power now, Tess thought as she drove, a man of great status, but Winston Sinclair would still help someone like her. Or rather *her* specifically. They had a past, a hot stormy history that had changed her life, at least for a while.

She'd been young when she met the dashing island man in Washington. He was handsome, polished, and on his way up the political ladder in Aruba. He'd come to the States to study the economy. They'd been introduced at a restaurant on Pennsylvania Avenue. Tess was in college at the time, but early on she'd developed a taste for the finer things and had found ways to support her expensive tastes.

The attraction between them had been instant—perhaps because they knew it couldn't last. Perhaps it was because he was married and a liaison between them was forbidden. Or maybe it was pure and simple passion. He was different from all the others. It was the first time she'd regarded a man as something more than a means to an end. A part of her fantasized that she and Winston could have a life together, that he could make an honest woman out of her. . . . But it was only fantasy.

Their affair lasted for six months, and then Winston returned to Aruba and Tess discovered she was pregnant.

Being young and in love, she convinced herself that she would become a single mom. She'd give up her "other life," and she'd love her love child with or without its dad in the picture.

"Pregnant!" her sister Tracy screeched when she'd called and told her the news. "Tess, are you crazy? You're only nineteen years old. You're going to fuck up your whole life."

"I want this baby, Tracy."

"What about a career? Your life?"

"I can make a life."

"Don't do this. You'll regret it."

"So I guess I don't have your support?"

"No. Not for this, Tess. It's a mistake."

"Thanks, Tracy." She'd hung up the phone and never spoke to her sister about it again.

Tracy was in New York attending Columbia University with aspirations of moving into law. Tess, on the other hand, was secretly hoping to find someone to care about her one day. Her deceased parents hadn't cared. It was clear since childhood that her fraternal twin, Tracy, was the favorite. Tracy could do no wrong. So of course she would think that this pregnancy was an atrocity.

So Tess decided to go it alone. She knew it was pointless to tell Winston. He would never leave his wife for some teenager. But in the end, she'd done what was best for her and the child. She'd never felt like that about a man again . . . until Vincent.

TESS DROVE SLOWLY up the long winding driveway, ringed on either side by towering willow trees. A few lights dotted the windows of the vast estate. She approached the entry gate and waited.

"Yes," came the sudden terse squawk from the intercom.

"Tess McDonald. I'm here to see the prime minister."

The gate opened immediately. Since her arrival on the island, Tess was a frequent and favored visitor to the private home of the island's prime minister. She hoped that relationship would pay off now.

The heavy wrought-iron gate slowly parted. She drove along the lane toward the front door and then around to the back of the house. She pressed her fingers to Vincent's throat. His pulse was weak, and his breath had grown increasingly sharp and raspy.

Tess grabbed her purse, got out of the car, and locked the doors. She hurried around to the front of the house, dashing through the rain.

Earl, the butler, was waiting. "Ms. McDonald, was the PM expecting you?"

"No. But it's urgent that I see him," she said, a bit breathless. She wiped water from her face.

"He has guests in the study. Come in out of the rain. I'll see if he can be disturbed."

"No! I mean no, I'll wait here. It's rude enough of me that I came without calling first. But please impress upon him that it's urgent."

Earl peered at her through the shadows and then nodded before walking back into the house.

Tess stole a glance over her shoulder. The seconds that passed after Earl's exit seemed interminable.

When Winston appeared at the door, he was as dapper and handsome as always. Winston epitomized the "stately gentleman," from his imposing six-foot-four height and solid two-hundred-pound weight to his smooth olive complected face, framed in salt-and-pepper hair and tapered beard. But appearances were truly deceiving. For all his outward pomp, behind closed doors, Winston Sinclair was an insatiable animal who gave as good as he got.

"Tess. My gawd, what on earth are you doing out in this weather? Come in." He extended his hand.

Tess grabbed it. "I can't. But I need your help."

TWO

THE GUESTS back at Tess's villa on the other side of the island began to take their leave. The party had been a stellar success, despite Tess's obvious absence. The stunning array of women whom Tess had handpicked for her new entourage had effectively charmed the men of money and power in attendance. They'd come in all their finery, flaunting their wealth and prestige, forging new liaisons that would be beneficial for all concerned.

Kimberly Shepherd-Benning and Nicole Perez couldn't have been more pleased. The move from New York had been well worth it.

They'd both left behind the ugly deeds of their pasts. This was the chance that Tess promised, a chance for a very lucrative future.

"So what do you think?" Nicole asked Kim as they walked together into the main room, drinks in hand. The white-tuxedoed combo played light jazz with a reggae beat in the background.

"I think Tess is a brilliant, manipulative businesswoman with vision."

"You admire that, don't you?"

Kim turned to Nicole. "Of course. Don't you?" She took a sip from her glass and waved to a departing guest.

"I admire power," Nicole said in a light Hispanic accent. "This is an opportunity for me to have some of my own." She watched the men from beneath a veil of dense black lashes; her onyx hair hung in a thick ponytail that caressed her lower back. Money flowed from the assemblage as fluidly as the drinks flowed into them, she observed. That knowledge suffused her like adrenaline. She'd spent the better part of her life poor and struggling, always at the mercy of others. She'd saved as much as she could from the fast and furious days of the car heists she'd pulled with Trust— *God condemn his soul to hell.*

But now the door was open to fortunes she'd only dreamed of. To think, none of this would have been possible had Tess not opened the Pandora's box of revenge that steamy summer night during the New York City blackout. After hours of being trapped together on an elevator, the three strangers—Tess, Nicole, and Kim—became unlikely partners in unspeakable crimes. With no transportation in or out of the city, the trio made its way to Kimberly's standing hotel room on Seventh Avenue. . . .

BY THE TIME *the second bottle of brandy was finished, the three women had shared stories of their early beginnings, their struggles and triumphs. More important, they shared the minute details of the objects of their hatred—from their habits to their hangout spots to their associates. They laughed, they cried, they drank some more, wallowing in their* anger and misery, giving in to that dark untapped place in their souls and buoyed by the power of one common objective: retribution.

"I have an idea," Tess slurred.

"No more ideas from you," Nicole said, her accent thick and stilted. She giggled.

"Gimme a piece of paper, Kim."

Kim looked at Tess through bleary eyes. "Not . . . getting up . . . get it yourself. Next to the bed." She leaned her head back against the seat of the couch and closed her eyes.

Tess pushed herself up off the floor with the help of a good shove from Nicole and stumbled into the bedroom. She sat down on the side of the bed and opened the nightstand drawer.

On each of three slips of paper she wrote a single name and stuck them in separate envelopes, then sealed the envelopes.

"Tell you what," she said, reentering the living room, her words trailing behind her. "I'm going to put these envelopes on the bar. Everybody gets one."

"What's in 'em?" Nicole asked. "Money?" She snickered.

"The name of the person you're going to kill, silly."

Kim burst out laughing and slapped her thigh. "Like a Secret Santa!" She cracked up laughing again.

"I know my vision is kinda cloudy, but I can count. That's four envelopes." Nicole frowned. "Who else is playing?"

"The fourth one is blank." Tess looked at them. "One of us may be lucky enough to get it." Tess waited a beat. "It's like a game of Russian roulette. Who wants to play? Who's woman enough? Who wants to make them pay for screwing up our lives?"

"I do!" Nicole managed to get up off the floor and staggered over to the counter. She stared at the envelopes. After several moments of indecision, she picked one and returned to her space on the couch. She stared at

Kim. "Well, whatcha waiting for, Christmas?" She jerked her chin toward the counter. "Maybe you'll get lucky and get the blank one. You don't have the heart to do anything bigger than signing checks for the leech husband of yours anyway." She started to laugh and couldn't stop.

"Fuck you," Kim said with such regal elocution, it shut Nicole up in midchuckle.

Tess covered her mouth, but that didn't stop her burst of laughter. "Didn't think you had it in you."

Kim walked to the counter with as much dignity as she could summon and snatched up an envelope without a second thought. She tossed Nicole a look of triumph and a haughty lift of her chin.

"Guess that leaves me." The contents of her stomach suddenly rose to her throat. What was she doing? This was crazy, a deadly game. But she knew they would never go through with it anyway. It was just a drunken game. She gripped the side of the counter to keep from falling. A crooked smile distorted the smooth lines of her face.

"What happens to the last envelope?" Kim asked.

"Burn it," Nicole said. "Give it here. I'll do it."

Tess tossed her the envelope. Nicole held it over the flame from the candle, and they all watched the paper curl, burn, and disintegrate into ash.

"We can really do this," Kim said, as if the idea had finally come together in her mind.

"You damned right we can." Nicole polished off her drink.

Kim shifted her body. "I think it's the perfect solution to our problems," Kim said, moving into CEO mode. "There's no connection between any of us. But we must keep it that way."

AND THEY HAD, Nikki mused, staring out upon the expanse of cloudy skies and rippling water. Those envelopes contained the names of Tracy Alexander, Tess's sister; Troy Benning, Kimberly's husband; and Trust Lang, her ex-lover. All gone for good.

"So, ladies, what did you think of our little soiree?"

Kim and Nicole turned at the voice behind them. Charrie stood there with a satisfied smile on her face. Naturally curly hair sat like a glistening cap on her head. Tiny diamond studs dotted her lobes.

"I couldn't have done better myself," Kimberly said.

"I'm sure Tess will be happy to hear that."

"Where is she, anyhow?" Nicole asked. "She's been gone for a while."

"Tess is her own woman," Charrie said, glancing away for a moment. "I'm sure she'll be back when she's ready."

"I see you've changed outfits," Kim commented.

Charrie glanced down at her halter dress. "Yes." She laughed lightly. "Didn't want to bore anyone." She blew out a sigh. "Well, if you'll excuse me, I want to say good night to the last of the guests." She walked away.

"She's damned sure of herself," Nicole groused.

"Maybe she has reason to be. Tess trusts her. They've worked together for a long time."

"So where do we fit in?"

Kim cut Nicole a look. "At the top. Where we belong. Where we were promised."

"I don't like her," Nicole said, staring at Charrie's bare back. "There's something about her that bugs me."

"Well, be sure to keep your personal issues to yourself. I'm not going to have you screw things up for me."

"Fuck you, *chica*."

Kim grinned and walked away.

Nicole watched Charrie charm one of the men Nikki'd met earlier. He was a local bank president, married and very wealthy. Charrie had her hand on his thigh as she arched her long neck in soft laughter.

Nicole sipped her drink. She didn't like the bitch. Not one fuckin' bit. And her instincts were never wrong.

KIM WENT UPSTAIRS to her bedroom. She was exhausted. *Bone-weary* would be a better word. She kicked off her shoes and went straight to the bathroom to turn on the shower. At the sink she splashed cool water on her face as the room slowly filled with steam. Lifting her head, she met her foggy reflection in the faux gold–framed mirror.

In a year's time, she'd gone from being CEO of Shepherd Enterprises—one of the most thriving businesses on Wall Street—to being a murderer who'd lost almost her entire fortune. Only to arrive on the sandy beaches of Aruba to help head up an elite escort service for the very same woman who'd conceived of the deadly plan to get rid of her trifling husband, Troy Benning.

"Life's a bitch and then you die," she murmured to her reflection, no longer recognizing the woman in the mirror.

Desperation had driven her to agree to Tess's pact. *No one would ever know. Murder by stranger happens every day.* Tess's fateful words rang in her head.

Tess had been right. The death of her husband, Troy, had been deemed a tragic accident, but Kim knew better. Her conscience wouldn't allow her to forget. And she also knew that it had to be Nikki who'd made Troy's death appear like an unfortunate car accident. Hadn't she bragged about her skills with cars while they were trapped in the elevator?

Kim turned away from the damning reflection, afraid she'd see visions of the night she sent Trust hurtling over his own balcony to his death.

Yes, hers and Nicole's enemies had been disposed of. But what kept her up at night was the idea of the name in the third envelope—Tracy Alexander—Tess's sister.

Tess must have picked her sister's name from the envelopes. And if Tess could kill her sister to save herself, then Tess McDonald was capable of anything. To someone else, that might be a chilling thought, Kim mused as she stepped under the beating water. Not to her. She knew that she was capable of anything as well.

NICOLE WANDERED OUT BACK and had a seat on the wooden bench overlooking a magnificent tropical garden. The sudden and violent thunderstorm had left the air smelling sweet and new.

She set her glass down next to her and took out a pack of Newports from her black beaded purse.

It would be easy to get used to this life, Nicole thought, blowing a puff of smoke into the air.

She was a long way from East Harlem. A long way from the ratty two-bedroom apartment she'd shared with her older brother and younger sister. A long way from the eighteen months of her life lost in a jail cell.

Nicole tugged in a lungful of smoke. The nightmare of what happened to her behind those metal bars still crept up on her, grabbed her by the throat, and tried to choke the breath from her body. Only her unwavering desire to see Trust pay for what he did to her had kept her sane, kept her praying for the day she would be free.

He had been her everything: her boss, her mentor, her lover, and ultimately her betrayer. He turned her on to the fast life of the street and the quick money. He turned her out from an inexperienced young woman into one who knew her body, knew how to use it and how to get what she wanted with it.

She'd loved Trust. Loved him with her entire being. She'd lost her family because of him, sacrificed her innocence and a chunk of her life. And hell hath no fury like a woman betrayed. Trust had betrayed her love, her loyalty, and her devotion. Therefore, he had paid the ultimate price.

She ground out her cigarette. The only regret she had was that she hadn't seen the look on his face as he went sailing through the air.

Nikki pushed herself up to her feet. She surveyed her new world. She would be wealthy, she'd travel, she'd entertain powerful men. And one day she would find her sister and brother and make it all up to them. But first, she'd have to find a way to replace Charrie as Tess's right hand and confidante. She smiled. It was only a matter of time.

THREE

WINSTON PEERED INTO THE DARKENED VEHICLE then quickly jerked back. He whirled toward Tess. "What the hell? . . . He's been shot."

"I know. That's why I need your help."

"Tess, this man needs a doctor." He stole another quick look inside the car. Vincent moaned.

"I can't take him to a doctor *or* a hospital."

Winston stared at her. "What have you done?"

"I don't want to involve you any more than necessary."

"Involve me!" His voice rose with indignation. "You involved me the minute you drove onto my property."

"Winston . . ." She stepped up to him, looked directly into his sea green eyes, trying to evoke the memories between them. She placed her hand on his stiff bicep. "I have nowhere else to turn.

You know if I could, I would. If anyone can get him the help he needs—discreetly—it's you." She paused a beat. "Please."

Winston twisted his full lips, his gaze boring into hers. Tess had brought him hours of pleasure and excitement, in the bedroom and out of it. He had thought himself in love with her once upon a time, but he knew that was foolish. A man of his position could not be publicly involved with a woman like Tess McDonald, no matter how beautiful, intelligent, and sexy.

"Drive the car down to the guesthouse." Winston rounded the car and got into the passenger seat.

"Thank you, Winston," she said on a breath of relief. She quickly got into the car and eased it farther down the drive, behind a cove a trees until she reached the guesthouse. Winston got out first, briskly walking to the front door. He took a quick look around, as if expecting someone to jump out of the rainy shadows and point an accusing finger.

He fished around the top of the doorframe and located the spare key then unlocked the door. He pushed the door open, returned to the car, and with Tess's help they carried the leaden body into the house.

"Put him down over here," Winston said, backing his way toward the couch.

They set Vincent down.

Tess knelt next to Vincent. She touched his forehead and then looked up at Winston, panic lighting her eyes. "He's ice cold."

"I'll get some blankets. He's probably going into shock." Winston darted to the back of the house.

"Vincent, I'm so sorry. This should never have happened." She stroked his forehead. "Please don't die on me. We're going to get you help, and I swear to you I'll explain everything."

Winston returned, his arms loaded with blankets. "Here, take these. I'm going to call for some help."

Tess took the blankets and started tucking them around Vincent's body. "Is it someone you can trust?" She glanced upward toward Winston.

"I only deal with people that I can trust." He walked out of the room to the back.

Tess focused on Vincent. His chestnut face seemed drained of color. His lids flickered, and for a moment, Tess thought he would open them. He didn't. Tenderly she stroked his brow and then his cheeks.

"Who is he to you, Tess?"

She turned, wiping any semblance of emotion from her face. She offered Winston a wan smile. "A friend."

Winston chuckled deep in his throat. "I know the kind of friends you have, my dear." He stared right at her. She didn't flinch. "Someone will be here shortly. Keep him warm, and pray he doesn't die on us in the meantime." He walked to the front door. "I still have guests. I'll be back."

"Thank you, Winston," she said softly.

Winston gave her a curt nod, opened the door, and walked out, closing it firmly behind him.

Tess eased down onto the floor and curled her legs beneath her, all the while holding Vincent's unresponsive hand. What the hell had happened? It shouldn't have gone down like this. True, she had set out with the intention of shooting him—if necessary. But intending to and actually having it happen were two entirely different things.

The minutes dragged on. Where was the doctor? She got up and went to the window, daring to peek out from behind the wooden blinds. In the distance she could see the lights from the main house twinkling from between the trees. She frowned, concentrating on the moment when it all went to hell. It had happened so fast.

She'd slowed her car to a stop and turned off her headlights, taken her gun from her purse, and switched off the safety. The moment she'd stepped out of the car, she'd noticed movement to her right. Vincent stepped out, his silhouette outlined by the moon. She'd know him anywhere, even in the dead of night on foreign shores. Her heart pounded with anticipation and a need she hadn't felt since she was last in his bed.

She'd stood stock still. Vincent moved toward her. That panther stride unmistakable. Her gun hand shook.

Then two short pops, and Vincent crumbled to the ground.

A soft knock jerked her away from the window. She'd been so caught in the recollection, she hadn't seen anyone approach. She went to the door.

"Yes?"

"Winston sent me."

Tess eased the door open and faced a tall distinguished man who looked more like a college professor than a doctor.

"I'm Dr. Braithwaite," he said with a clear Caribbean accent that sounded more Bajan that Arubian.

"Please, come in. He's over there."

Dr. Braithwaite breezed by her and went directly to where Vincent lay. He touched the man's forehead and then gingerly peeled back the blanket. The right side of Vincent's shirt was soaked with blood. He shook his head and mumbled something that Tess could not hear. He pulled up Vincent's T-shirt, then reached in his bag for a pair of latex gloves.

"How long ago did this happen?" he asked as he gently examined the wound.

"About an hour ago."

He slipped his hands beneath Vincent and lifted him, looking for an exit wound. "Went clean through."

"Is that good?"

Dr. Braithwaite looked up at her over his shoulder. "No gunshot is good. But at least I won't have to dig it out. He's lost a great deal of blood. That's my main concern—that and infection, of course." He stood and snapped off his gloves. "I'll have to move him to my office. Get the wound clean, put him on an IV, and get him stitched up."

Tess nodded.

Dr. Braithwaite faced her. "Two thousand up front, in cash."

Tess blanched. "I don't have that kind of money on me."

He shrugged his left shoulder. "When you get it—" He tossed a look over his shoulder. "—I'll be more than happy to help you."

Tess lifted her chin. "So much for the Hippocratic oath," she said, her tone even. "You'd actually let a man die for money?"

"If you could take this man to a hospital, I would think you would have done so. Am I right?"

She didn't respond. Being on the wrong end of a deal was never part of her game plan. Now wasn't the time to start.

"I'll get the money for you. That's not a problem. You take care of him. I'll take care of you. You have my word."

"And mine."

They both turned to the door.

Winston stood in the threshold. "Do what you need to do, Clem. You'll get your money." Winston stepped inside. "I'd hate to initiate an investigation into your medical practice," he added calmly, punctuating his comment with a wry smile.

Clem's Adam's apple bobbed for a moment while his nostrils flared. "Help me get him to the car."

FOUR

THE ROOM WAS WINDOWLESS, narrow, and sterile, devoid of any fur-
nishings other than the utilitarian hospital bed, a rolling cart lined
with medical tools, an IV stand, and the sinfully hard leather chair
that she'd spent the past three days sitting in.

There was a tiny bathroom behind an almost invisible door,
where she was able to take a bird bath. The doctor dropped in
twice per day to check on his patient and to bring her food and
water. Other than that, it was just her and Vincent.

She hadn't left the room or Vincent's side since they'd brought
him in. Dr. Braithwaite warned that it might be days before he
woke up. That had been three days earlier. Between the loss of
blood and the shock that his body endured, the longer Vincent
stayed unconscious, the better his chances for healing.

Every bone in Tess's body screamed in agony. She ached from

the top of her head to the bottoms of her feet. Slowly she pushed herself up to a standing position, pressed her palms to her lower back, and arched; then she twisted gingerly from side to side.

She'd tried several times to contact Charrie on the phone, but she got no signal on her cell. No telling what they were thinking might have happened to her. But Tess knew that Charrie could handle any situation, and whatever inquiries she made as to her whereabouts would be totally discreet.

She'd thought several times of asking Dr. Braithwaite to get a message to her, but his cold-shouldered indifference held her off. Tess could tell that he was still irked by the fact that Winston backed her up and went so far as to threaten the good doctor. He didn't take that well. And although he did his doctorly duty regarding Vincent, it was clear that he had a blatant dislike for her. The less she had to ask of him, the better. She'd figure something out. She always did.

Vincent stirred and moaned lightly. Tess hurried to his side. His lids fluttered. He opened his eyes and then slowly closed them, as if keeping them open was a struggle. He tried to move and groaned at the effort, his handsome face contorting in pain.

Tess put her hand on his shoulder. "Ssssh, take it easy. Try not to move around."

His eyes slowly opened. His features were tight and drawn. It took a minute for him to focus on her face. His nostrils flared. "Slipping something into . . . my IV?" he asked, his voice thick and raspy. "Finishing me off?"

"Now is not the time," she said, sidestepping his comment. "You were hurt pretty bad. You need your rest."

"Why are you here?"

"I wanted to make sure you were all right."

He turned his head slowly from side to side. "Where the hell am I?"

"The doctor brought you here, cleaned up your wound, and stitched you up."

Vincent started to cough.

Tess picked up a glass of water from the rolling table, lifted his head, and brought the glass to his lips. "Slowly," she warned.

He sipped greedily and then turned his head away. Tess put the glass down and turned to him.

"You didn't answer my question. You come to finish me off?"

"No. I was the one who got you help."

"Why?"

For a moment she faltered. Flashes of Vincent lying in the street, blood oozing from his side, leaped before her eyes. She shook the images away with a slight toss of her head. "Maybe I had an attack of conscience."

"You?" He tried to laugh but winced instead. "I was pretty sure you didn't have one of those."

"You don't know me."

He looked right into her eyes. "You're wrong. I do know you, Tess. You're driven by greed, power, and your ability to bend others to your will. You'll stop at nothing to accomplish your goals. Nothing. You have no soul, no heart. That's what I know about you."

She took a step back, the impact of his words digging a deep gouge in her heart. He was so wrong. So very wrong. But this wasn't about her. Not now. This was about getting him well.

"Since we're being all honest, why don't I tell you what I know about you." She stepped up to the bed and grasped the metal railing. "You're full of shit. You're no better than me. You use people to get what you want. You crept into my life, into my bed, between my legs to get what you wanted—information about me and my business to ruin me and to further your own career and line your pockets. You pretended to be something you have no clue about being—human."

"Is that why you shot me?" he retorted. "'Cause you were pissed that someone so full of shit as me had figured you all out?"

Tess whirled away and walked over to the chair. She snatched up her purse and pulled out his .45 to wave it in front of him. She jerked up her chin, the fire in her eyes meeting his. "Actually, it sounds more like something you would do." She waited a beat. "You would have shot me had you gotten the chance," she said, but even as she did, a part of her hoped that he would deny the accusation.

"Why did you leave without a word?" he asked, his tone suddenly low and intimate. It caught her off guard.

She swallowed down the truth—that she loved him and could not bear to see the look in his eyes when he put everything together—the fact that he knew who she was and how she made her living. In a back corner of her soul, it mattered to her what Vincent thought of her. Their hot but short-lived romance was her fantasy—a life away from "the life." And the insertion of truth ruined it all.

She pushed out a breath and returned the gun to her purse. "It doesn't matter now."

"It does to me."

"Why? Tell me why you'd give a damn if I hung around or not?"

His chest heaved in and out. The silence hung between them like a velvet curtain. He swallowed. "You're right." He turned his head away. "It doesn't matter."

A weight leveled itself in her stomach. "As long as we're clear," she said.

Vincent tried to sit up. Instinctively Tess moved to help him, but stopped midway. Instead she walked to the other side of the empty room and leaned against the wall.

"How long . . ."

She looked up from staring at her feet. "What?"

"How long have I been here?"

"Three days."

He turned to her with a frown creasing his features. "You've . . . been here the whole time?"

She nodded and then looked away.

He ran his tongue over dry lips. "Why?"

She jerked her head in his direction. "Why what, Vincent? Why didn't I just let you die in a pool of your own blood in the dirty street? Why did I use my resources to get you help? Why have I sat here for three days, wiping your sweat, checking your IV, and hoping that you'd finally wake up? Are those the whys you want answers to?"

"Yeah, I do."

A sarcastic grin lifted the right corner of her mouth. "Like we agreed, Vincent, it doesn't matter. And if you can't figure it out on your own, then it *really* doesn't." She crossed the room, snatched up her purse from the chair, and headed for the door. "The doctor comes twice a day. He'll bring you something to eat. And I'm sure when he thinks you're ready, he'll let you go." She opened the door. "I left you alone. I'd be honored if you would afford me the same courtesy." Tess arched a defiant brow and offered a sad smile; then she opened the door and stepped out into the cool afternoon.

"Tess," he whispered.

She didn't hear him. The door shut behind her.

Vincent flopped back down onto the thin mattress. He squeezed his eyes shut as hot pain ran along his side. He touched the bandages that covered his right side from front to back. *Bullet must have gone clean through.* He drew in a deep breath then forced himself to sit up. He reached down the side of the bed, searching for the lever to lower the guardrail. After several attempts, the railing dropped. With great effort he sent his legs toward the floor and tried to stand. He had to find her. This wasn't over.

That was the last thing he remembered.

Five

IT HAD BEEN nearly a year. On the surface, her life was what could be considered normal. She shopped at the local grocer, attended church with her neighbors on Sundays, strolled the malls, visited the museums, and even took in a movie from time to time. Her small two-bedroom home was cozy, with a majestic view of the Rocky Mountains in the distance. She even had a male friend, Mark Drayton, whom she allowed to warm her on some nights when she felt especially lonely. He knew her only as Victoria Styles, a young widow who'd relocated to get away from the memories of her husband's loss during 9/11. What he knew was enough.

She hadn't told Avery about Mark. Avery would strongly disapprove. He'd warned her about becoming too attached to anything or anyone in the event that she had to be moved again or that the someone getting close was really there to finish what they'd started. At times she was uncertain if it was the district attorney worried about her well-being or if it was Avery Powell, the man. In any event, it did her no good to ponder it either way. She and Avery were over and done a long time ago.

By day she worked part-time at the local library, shelving books and reading to kids three days per week. The rest of the time, she did what she did best.

She heard a rustle at the front door. For an instant, her entire body went on alert before realizing that it was only the mailman pushing the mail through the slot. Her heart slowed. She should be used to it by now—this normal way of life. But that one night still haunted her.

She picked up the mail from the floor and flipped through it. Avery had insisted that she get a P.O. box, but she fought him and won on that count. If she was going to live like everyone else—at least on the surface—she wanted to get her mail like everyone else in her small suburban community.

The last thick envelope, with no return address, was the one she'd been expecting. Postmarked from New York. She walked into her living room, sat down on her used couch, and opened it.

She and Avery had decided that if she was going to continue to work in any capacity, using the good old U.S. mail was the best way for her to receive her assignments. Although the Internet was faster, it was also vulnerable to hackers. Anything done on the Internet could be traced, no matter how well they thought they'd covered their tracks. Discovery was something they could ill afford to happen.

She opened the thick wad of folded documents and reviewed them one page at a time. He'd sent her background information on two old cases. One was the death of Troy Benning, husband to media mogul Kimberly Shepherd-Benning. *Interesting*. The other was the apparent gang-related murder of a Trust Lang, a known drug dealer, among other things.

She vaguely recalled hearing about Benning in some sort of car accident. But she'd already been squirreled away by then. So the details were sketchy. The other she knew nothing about. Why would Avery have her waste time looking into the death of some gang member?

She studied the documents again then walked into her bedroom to get her cell phone. She dialed the special number she'd been given and waited for the call to connect. Moments later, Avery Powell was on the line.

"Is everything all right?" he said instead of a standard greeting. They'd agreed that the phone would be used sparingly and only if it was urgent.

"Everything is fine." She heard his breath of relief.

"I got the information today."

"Good. I assume you either have a problem or a question."

"What made you pick these cases? I don't see anything in there that warrants me looking into them."

"Let's just say I have my suspicions, particularly with Troy Benning. He helped run Shepherd Enterprises, or so it appears on paper. With him out of the way, Mrs. Shepherd-Benning had a clear playing field to all the money, but the company almost went belly-up. She let go of staff, closed down divisions. It's less than half of what it used to be, and the biggest kicker of them all is that dear Mrs. Shepherd-Benning has disappeared."

"Disappeared as in tragically or of her own free will?"

"That's what I want you to find out."

"So what about this other guy, Trust? Who cares?"

"That's the other thing. There was a minimal investigation at best. From what we can tell, his business associate, Monroe, has taken over, although we can't quite pin anything on him. However, he had a girlfriend. It's in the notes. . . ."

She flipped through the pages. "A, uh, Nikki Perez."

"Right. Well, it seems that she's done the bird, too."

She frowned. "I can't imagine that there's any connection. . . ." Her voice and thought drifted off.

"That's what I thought at first. Totally unrelated . . ."

"Making them more related than they appear."

"Exactly."

She leaned back against the cushion of the couch, running what information she had through her head. It was definitely a puzzle—an interesting one.

"There's no rush on this," Avery said. "Take whatever time you need."

"Right." His sarcasm wasn't lost on her. To Avery, "take your time" meant just the opposite. And he always expected results.

"How are things with you?"

She sighed. "Dull and safe."

Avery chuckled. "Excellent."

"And you?"

"Just the opposite. Well, I'd better go. I have a press conference in twenty minutes."

"I'll start working on this."

"Thanks, Tracy . . . I mean . . . Victoria."

"It's good to hear my real name from time to time."

"As long as it's me saying it."

"Take care, Avery."

"By the way, your sister has disappeared, too."

Avery slowly hung up the phone. He knew it was underhanded to toss the bait at Tracy like that. But he knew that she would take it, just like Vincent did. Both of them, once they got the scent, were unstoppable. Avery would get what he wanted in the end. And he'd do it the easy way: by having others do it for him.

Tracy owed him. It may not be the life she wanted, but at least it was a life. He'd made that possible.

The night of her attempted assassination was a night of whirlwind action and split-second decision making. When he arrived at the hospital, Tracy was already on the operating table. The police were out in force, both to barricade the hospital from the onslaught of the media as well as to protect ADA Tracy Alexander from another attempt.

The instant Avery arrived on the scene, he was met by the police commissioner.

"What the hell happened, Carl?" Avery growled, meeting the commissioner stride for stride as they hurried along the hospital corridor.

"Best we can tell is that someone came up on her, shot her point-blank in the chest."

Avery pressed his palm to his forehead. "Christ! Any word?" He turned to Carl, his gaze boring into the man like a drill bit.

"Doctor says it's serious. That's all I know. That and that there was a helluva lot of blood."

Avery's jaw clenched. He and Tracy had worked together for years, in the office and in the bedroom, the latter association burning itself out over time. They'd butted heads over cases, and he knew he'd used his clout and his position as her boss to keep her in her place. He'd had moments when he wanted her out of the department, flat on her ass with nowhere else to go. But this. Never this.

"We're pretty sure it was a hit, Avery."

He nodded absently. "Of course it was. She just sent away the most notable drug lord this side of Colombia."

They both sat down on a bench just outside the operating room, keeping a watchful eye on the swinging doors.

"How do you want to handle this?" Carl asked.

"We keep a lid on this. A tight one. No one talks to the media unless I give the okay. I approve every comment. They all come through my office."

"Done."

"What if she makes it?"

"If she makes it . . . no one will ever know."

Carl nodded solemnly, understanding the implications. "I'll get in touch with the FBI and put the pieces in motion, just in case we need to use them."

Avery rocked his jaw back and forth. "Thanks."

It was nearly three hours later before the surgeon emerged from the operating room.

He pulled his cap from his head and walked over to Avery and Carl. They both rose as he approached.

"She's lucky. And tough. She lost a lot of blood. If she can get through the next forty-eight hours, she has a chance. The bullet just missed her heart and her spine."

Avery shut his eyes for a moment, then focused on the doctor. "How soon can she be moved?"

"She's in critical condition. I wouldn't risk moving her for a least a week, and that all depends on the next two days."

"We have to get her out of here before then. I can have her flown out."

"I can't approve something like that. I—"

Avery held up his hand. "I'll take full responsibility." He shot Carl a look and then put his hand on the doctor's shoulder. "Is there someplace where we can talk privately?"

The doctor's eyes darted from one face to the other. "Uh, in my office."

Avery stared at the plaques on his office wall. That night seemed like an eternity ago. They'd staged Tracy's funeral, even had a body double in her casket. All the while, she was recovering from her injuries hundreds of miles away in Colorado. For all intents and purposes, Assistant District Attorney Tracy Alexander was dead and buried. In order for her to stay alive, everyone must continue to believe that she was dead. There were only two people who knew that she was alive and where she was, him and Special Agent Vincent Royal.

SIX

TESS HAD EVERY INTENTION of returning to her villa. By now, even Charrie would be worried. However, the more she thought about it, the less it appealed as an option. Instead, she drove to the farthest end of the island and parked on a hilltop overlooking the ocean. She'd taken a towel from Dr. Braithwaite's hideaway office to temporarily cover up the bloodstain in the car. She didn't dare ask Winston for any more help. She'd figure it out.

She stepped out of the car and walked up the slope of the hill. She drew in a deep breath and gazed down at the crystal blue water below.

What she needed was a plan. Vincent was alive, and at some point he would be well enough to come after her again. Running for the rest of her life was not an option; neither was prison. She paced across the emerald green grass and even lifted her head to the heavens, wistfully imagining that the answers would rain down on her. If only it were that simple.

She lowered herself to the grassy knoll and drew her knees up to her chest. Maybe she should call Charrie and tell her and everyone else to get the hell out of there. Vincent, for all his machismo, wasn't strong enough to launch an all-out attack on her and her business. But in short order he would be.

She tugged on her bottom lip with her teeth and watched a seagull soar over the water then dive beneath the depths only to appear moments later with a flapping fish clenched in its bill. The analogy of it to her own life wasn't lost on her. Vincent was the gull, out on the hunt, and if she didn't dive deep enough, he was sure to snatch her up and devour her.

This was between the two of them. It was *her* that he wanted, *not* the business—of that she was certain. If she left now, left a trail that he was sure to follow, she could lead him away from the business and keep the ladies safe.

She had money stashed that she could get to, and she had influential friends that could get her out of Aruba. But where would she go, and just how much of her scent did she want to leave behind?

CHARRIE'S BACK WAS to the door. She was just hanging up the phone when Kim walked into the room.

"Any word from Tess?"

Charrie jumped and spun toward Kim. She pressed her hand to her chest. "Scared the shit out of me. I didn't hear you come in." She licked her lips and absentmindedly ran her fingers through her tight curls.

Kim walked fully into the room, her floral printed diaphanous dress and floor-length sleeveless jacket floated around her. Her blond hair was perfectly smoothed into a tight knot at the nape of her neck. Her makeup was flawless, her bearing regal. She looked every bit the woman of the house. Charrie took it all in.

The usually cool and in control Charrie seemed to have left the building for a moment, Kim noted. For an instant she looked more frightened than startled. Then, just as quickly, the polished woman Kim had come to know reappeared.

"Sorry, I should have knocked." She wandered over to the bay window and sat down on the window seat. She crossed her legs and rocked her right sandaled foot. "Still no word from Tess?"

"No."

"Have you tried her cell phone?"

"The recording says that she's out of range," Charrie said smoothly.

"You don't seem too concerned. It's been three days already, going on four. Don't you think you should call the police?"

"You're kidding, of course. Maybe that's what you'd do in your world. Not ours." She lifted her chin and stared hard at Kim.

Kim pursed her lips. If this *was* her world, she'd get that smug look of superiority off Charrie's face so fast, her head would spin. All it would take was a simple phone call. But as much as she hated to admit it, Charrie was right. This was all new territory to her. In her world of corporate shenanigans, she'd been the head bitch in charge. She'd had the power and used it at will. She knew all the players, their strengths and weaknesses. Here . . . it was a different story.

"So what do you plan to do in the meantime?"

"Exactly what Tess would expect—run the business." She

reached for her wineglass, which sat on the wicker-and-glass table-top and took a slow sip of something pink and bubbly.

"At some point I'm sure you'll fill us in, since Tess didn't have much of a chance to do so."

"Of course. Why don't you just relax for now, enjoy the down-time. Perhaps you and Nicole would like to see some of the sights. I can arrange it for you."

"Thanks. I'll let you know." She stood and walked to the door, then stopped midway and turned back to Charrie. "If, let's say, something unfortunate happened to Tess, that would leave you in charge of everything, wouldn't it?"

Charrie hesitated for an instant. "Yes, it would. But I'm sure Tess is fine and she'll return when she's ready. She always does."

Kim ran her glance along Charrie's model frame before set-tling on her face. "I'm sure." She turned and walked out.

Kim wandered out to the gazebo behind the house. Several women from the night of the party were lounging around the pool in varying stages of undress.

She felt her body grow warm as her eyes meandered along the soft curves, smooth skin, sinewy legs, and perfect breasts. She had not allowed herself the luxury of passion or desire since Stephanie—and certainly not since the death of her husband, Troy. She knew herself to be a highly sexual being, her carnal needs kept in check only by her equally demanding need to con-trol her empire. With Shepherd Enterprises at no more than a mere three hundred staffers at two office locations, the lid on her libido had been lifted.

It had taken all her self-control not to seek out one of the beau-ties the night of the party. But if she'd learned one thing as CEO of Shepherd Enterprises, it was that you don't mix business with pleasure, and you never try to undercut your employer unless you had the means to back it up. She'd be doing both if she made a move toward any of the women. Kim Shepherd may be a lot of things: a brilliant businesswoman, highly bisexual, rich, beautiful, and a murderer—but she wasn't stupid.

Kim strolled to the far end of the rectangular pool and stretched out on a pin-striped lounge chair. She had an excellent view of the ladies. If she couldn't play, at least she could fantasize. She slipped on her dark sunglasses and closed her eyes.

Did Stephanie miss her? she wondered. Did she ever think about her? They should have put Stephanie's husband's name in one of those damned envelopes. She smiled inwardly at the joke. But the truth was, when the cards were all spread out, Stephanie had chosen Malcolm over her, chosen her secure, high-profile life as a politician's wife. The rejection still stung. It hurt when she least expected it. She'd sacrificed her business, had her own husband murdered, all to protect Stephanie Abrams and her husband's career. And for what? Life's a bitch and then you die, she reminded herself.

"Napping or relaxing?"

Kim slowly removed her shades and squinted up into the sunlight. Gradually she made out the stunning image of Nicole standing above her. Nicole, for all her crude language and unsophisticated ways, was incredible to behold. Petite and voluptuous, with skin the color white girls spent hours trying to achieve. Midnight black eyes, lush lips, and a cascade of ebony hair that begged to be touched. Yes, she was all woman and definitely off-limits.

Kim sighed. "A bit of both."

Nicole looked around. "This is real beautiful and shit, but boring as hell." She pulled a pack of Newport cigarettes out of a tiny pocket on impossibly tight white shorts. She lit her cigarette and tossed the match carelessly to the ground.

Kim winced and shook her head. Beautiful and totally without a grain of class.

"Watch a movie, go for a swim," Kim offered with no real conviction. She put her shades back on, the better to look at Nicole without her noticing.

"I wanna see some sights." She leaned on her right leg, jutting her hip to the side, and blew a puff of noxious smoke into the air.

"Charrie offered to get someone to take us around."

Nicole snapped her head in Kim's direction. "Why didn't you say something?"

Kim shrugged.

"She say anything else; like where the fuck is Tess?"

"She said she still hasn't heard from her."

Nicole crouched down next to Kim and leaned close. "I don't like this shit. Somethin' ain't right."

Kim took off her shades again and pushed up on her elbows. "What do you mean?"

"I don't know exactly. Just got a bad vibe, ya know."

Kim was silent for a moment. She had the same unsettling feelings, but she'd attributed them to being in new surroundings, starting over. But Nicole speaking the words validated to her own apprehension.

"I've been thinking the same thing." She looked Nicole in the eyes. "Why would Tess bring us here only to vanish?"

"When she left, she said she had unfinished business—something to do with that guy she was seeing back in New York. Even though she didn't say it in so many words. But I can read in between the lines," she added as if it were a skill you earned a degree in.

"Listen, we told each other a crock of shit the night of the party. You know it, and so do I."

Nicole cocked a brow but didn't respond.

"Our hands are dirty. And the only one who knows about it is Tess."

"So whatchu sayin'?"

Kim exhaled long and slow. "I'm not sure."

"You think we're being set up?"

Kim's gaze snapped in Nicole's direction. "Do you?"

Nicole shrugged her right shoulder but kept her gaze locked on Kim. "Why doesn't Charrie want to look for Tess? If something happened to Tess, who wins? Charrie," she said, answering her own question.

"My thoughts exactly." Kim sat up fully. "And who's to say that Charrie would be as generous with us as Tess?"

"Told you I didn't like that bitch."

Kim held up her hand, offering another scenario. "But what if it's the other way around? Maybe Tess wants to get rid of all the loose ends once and for all." She lifted her brows. "Us."

Nicole frowned. "Naw." She stood up. "Tess ain't that kind of player. Why would she bring us all the way out here just to get rid of us?"

"Don't you see? Tess is a planner. She thinks out every inevitability. With us out there, the possibility of us being found out, maybe even breaking down and telling, was a possibility to her." Kim shook her head. "Tess couldn't let that happen. She's too smart. Think about it: Who knows where we are?" She stared at Nicole. "Nobody." Kim leaned closer to Nicole, briefly inhaled her soft scent. Her eyelids fluttered for an instant before she finally spoke in a whisper. "We need to find and get rid of Tess before she gets to us."

Nicole flinched and jerked back; then she suddenly burst out laughing. "You are one crazy white chick." She waved her hand in dismissal. "Hell naw. You're on your own, *chica*. My money is on Charrie." She formed her fingers into the shape of a gun and pointed it at the house. With that she turned and sashayed away.

Kim watched Nicole leave. It was too simple for Charrie to be behind Tess's sudden absence. They'd been together nearly a decade from what Tess told them. She was sure that Charrie must have had ample opportunities in the past to push Tess out and take over the reins. So why now? Makes no sense. Kim stared toward the blue water of the pool. No. It was Tess. She was sure of it now.

seven

DR. BRAITHWAITE TOOK HIS KEY from his shirt pocket and stuck it in the lock only to find the door already open. He hesitated for a moment before easing the door open.

The bed was empty.

He stepped inside. That's when he saw Vincent on the floor. He hurried over, knelt down, and pressed his fingers to Vincent's throat. He was still alive.

With great effort he got Vincent off the floor and back onto the bed. His wound was bleeding.

He pulled the medical cart next to the bed, then went to the sink to wash his hands. He put on a pair of latex gloves and gently removed the soaked bandage. He patted the area clean with gauze. Several of the stitches had broken.

What the hell had happened, and where was that woman,

Tess? He sterilized the affected area before putting in three more stitches. Vincent groaned, but he didn't wake up. Dr. Braithwaite covered the wound with clean dressing, hung a new IV bag, and locked the siderail on the bed.

He snapped off his gloves and ran the back of his hand across his damp forehead. What had he gotten himself involved in? That woman may be a friend of the PM, but she couldn't be worth him risking his medical license. The last thing he needed was to be faced with having to dispose of a dead body.

Winston Sinclair was a powerful man. But even he couldn't make certain things go away, and Clem had no intention of being left holding the bag.

Clem stared down at his patient. He'd wait until dark.

EIGHT

TRACY SAT ON THE COUCH with her legs curled beneath her, the documents spread out in front of her on the table. She'd been studying them for hours, moving the pages around like puzzle pieces, trying to make them fit. The police report detailing Troy Benning's fatal car accident, Trust's bizarre flight off his balcony, the downturn of Shepherd Enterprises, and the incarceration record of Nicole Perez.

Something kept nagging her about the whole thing. The lives that these women led would never have afforded them the opportunity to meet each other. They were from completely different worlds. Yet there was one common denominator; all the deaths happened within days of each other, including her own attempted assassination. And the women connected with the men were now missing in action. Coincidence?

And what of her sister, Tess? Avery said she was "missing" as well. Tess. Did Tess ever mourn her "death"? Did she ever realize that Tracy's final phone call to her had been to call a truce between them, let her know that she knew all about Tess being Madame X, but she was willing to destroy all the evidence in order to save her? Her heart ached.

She'd sacrificed her career for Tess, been willing to give it all up to save her sister from years in prison.

Tracy thought about that night often. Sometimes it would wake her from sleep. The shredding of documents . . . the phone call to Tess . . . her letter of resignation to Avery . . . the mysterious phone call to her office moments before she walked out of her office . . . a blast . . . a searing pain in her chest and her realizing that she was dying. Then . . . nothing.

Tracy sighed—a sudden loneliness seemed to swallow her whole. She lifted the glass of iced tea to her lips, tears stinging her eyes, just as her doorbell rang.

Her heart pounded. She sniffed hard and wiped at her eyes. Quickly she shuffled the papers together and shoved them in a folder then slid it under the couch. She stood and went to the door. She turned once, checking behind her to make sure she hadn't left anything out. She cleared her throat. "Who is it?"

"Special delivery," the voice called out.

She pushed out a breath and opened the door.

"Hi, sweetheart." Mark leaned down to give her a light kiss on the lips. "Thought I'd surprise you."

Mark Drayton was a good-looking man. Not handsome in the magazine kind of way, but easy on the eyes. He was of average height, about five feet eleven, thick build, but he kept himself in shape with jogging and skiing. He had a square solid jaw and warm brown skin. No beard or mustache. No scars or distinctive marks. To be truthful, Mark Drayton could be anyone. He was the kind of man who could easily blend into a crowd and never be noticed.

Tracy smiled. "And a pleasant one it is." She stepped aside. "Come on in."

"What were you up to?" he asked, walking into the living room.

Tracy's eyes immediately darted to the living room. The new James Patterson novel sat on the coffee table.

"Oh, nothing much, just reading." She locked the door and then followed him inside.

"I thought maybe we could go for a drive." He took off his heavy winter parka, revealing his broad chest. "It's beautiful out. Cold but clear. Then I thought we could see a movie and then dinner."

"Wow, what a lineup." She smiled, then plopped down on the couch next to Mark.

He dropped his arm around her shoulders and pulled her closer. "So is that a yes?"

Tracy looked up at him. "Yes. Sounds like what a girl needs on a Saturday."

"Great. Should I make reservations at that restaurant that we like, or do you want to wing it?"

"Let's wing. I'm feeling especially spontaneous today."

His brown eyes darkened. "Is that right?" He stroked the shoulder-length hair that hung loosely around her face. "How spontaneous?"

"Depends on what you have in mind," she said, her voice soft and inviting.

His index finger traced her bottom lip. She opened her mouth slightly and took it in, sucking gently.

"I've missed you, Victoria," he said, his voice suddenly thick. His free hand trailed along her collarbone down to the rise of her breasts. She drew in a sharp breath.

"Let's go upstairs," she said against the soft fabric of his metal-gray sweater. She got up and took his hand, leading him to her bedroom.

Mark wasn't the best lover she'd ever had, but he was sincere and thoughtful. She didn't experience "The Star-Spangled Banner" when they made love, but it helped to make her feel connected to something, to someone, at least for a little while.

As she lay naked beneath him, her knees bent, her thighs spread wide, she imagined for a moment that she was really happy and fulfilled, that she really was Victoria Styles, part-time library worker, and that the other person, ADA Tracy Alexander, was only a figment of her imagination.

While Mark pushed and pulled and she arched and rocked, she believed that it was exquisite, the best loving she'd ever had.

When his pace quickened and his breathing doubled, his thrusts grew more demanding, and words of endearment sprinkled down on her. She wrapped her legs around him, held him tight, and pretended that she was Victoria Styles.

"You don't talk much about your family," Mark said later that evening as they sat opposite each other at the restaurant.

Tracy focused on her steak as she cut into it. She shrugged slightly. "Not much to tell. It's just me."

"There has to be something." He put a piece of baked potato in his mouth and chewed thoughtfully while watching her. "You're so guarded."

Tracy's gaze rose. He was staring right at her. "I don't know what you mean." She reached for her glass of wine.

"Sure you do." He dug into his steak and cut slowly.

Tracy watched the way he held his knife, almost the way you would attack someone—it was tight in his fist. She knew the position, she'd demonstrated it more times than she would have liked during court cases. But she'd never noticed it about Mark until now.

"Why do you hold your knife like that?"

He stopped cutting his steak and held the knife up in his fist and looked at it as if noticing it for the first time. He frowned. "Old habit, I guess. When I was a kid, I worked summers at the ice house." He turned his gaze on Tracy. "You had to have a solid grip on the ice picks, or there could be some nasty accidents."

Tracy finally swallowed a mouthful of steak. A slight chill slid through her veins. She wasn't sure if her discomfort was caused by talking about ice on a chilly night or by something else. She blinked several times and forced a semblance of a smile.

"Oh," she murmured. "Makes sense."

He hadn't taken his eyes off her. "See, you found out something about me that I'd totally forgotten." He grinned and went back to eating. "Tell me again why you moved here."

"I, uh, needed to get away after I lost my husband."

"Right. He was a firefighter on 9/11. I know that part, but why here?"

"Here is far from there." She laughed lightly. "And far from everything familiar—the rush, the crowds, the skyscrapers, the noise, everything."

"Don't you miss your friends, your coworkers?"

"Not really. I was never much of a joiner."

"I'd think you would have made a lot of friends working for a law firm. The secretary pool is the hub of excitement." He flashed her a disarming grin. "At least that's what I've always heard."

"It can be, I suppose. But this was a very small firm." She added more French dressing to her salad.

Mark nodded then lifted his napkin and dabbed at his mouth. "All I want to do is get to know you, Vicky," he said softly. He reached across the table and took her hand. "If it seems like I'm prying, I'm sorry. It's just that sometimes I feel that I'm falling for a ghost. You're there and not there, ya know."

"I've always been a private person, Mark," she said as gently as she could. "Sometimes it's hard for me to open up." She paused for a beat. "I really want to put the past behind me. My life is here now."

He nodded slowly. "I understand, and I'll try to keep my questions to a minimum." He squeezed her hand. "Deal?"

"Deal."

"Dessert?"

The tension in her chest eased. "Of course."

They chatted of inconsequential things during dessert, and Tracy all but forgot the chilling feeling she'd had earlier.

Almost.

nine

DR. BRAITHWAITE PULLED UP to the front gate of Winston's home.
Earl's voice cracked through the intercom.

"It's Dr. Braithwaite," he answered.

The metal gate slowly opened and he drove through, but not
to the main house. He made the slight turn and headed for the
guesthouse beyond.

Once there, he cut the lights, got out of the car, and walked to
the main house. Earl was waiting for him on the front steps.

"I thought you'd gotten lost, sir."

"Is Winston available?" he asked rather than answer the indi-
rect question of what had taken him so long.

"He's in the study." Earl stepped aside to let Clem in. "If you'll
wait right here, I'll let the PM know that he has a guest."

Clem paced the gleaming wood floor, rehearsing in his mind

what he would say to Winston, determined not to back down no matter what threats Winston might issue.

Several moments later Winston appeared. "Clem. I wasn't expecting you."

"We need to talk. In private." His expression was resolute.

Winston glared at him for a moment, drew in a breath that puffed out his chest. "In my study."

Clem followed him down a short hallway and then turned right. Winston opened the study door. Clem stepped inside.

Winston shut the door. "What is it?"

Clem turned to face him. "We've been friends for a long time, Winston. I owe you my career." He shook his head. "But this favor you've asked of me isn't worth the two thousand dollars. It isn't worth all the money you could offer."

"What the hell are you saying, man? Get to the point."

"Your associate or whoever he is to you is in my car parked in front of the your guesthouse."

"What! Are you mad?" He darted to the window and pulled the curtains aside. He peered into the darkness and barely made out the silhouette of an automobile. He whirled toward Clem. "I paid you to take care of this, not to deposit it on my doorstep."

"Maybe you need to take that up with your lady friend, who seems to have disappeared."

Winston frowned. "Disappeared?"

"Yes. I came back to where I had him this afternoon, and she was gone. I found him on the floor."

Winston ran a hand across his chin and began to pace. "She wouldn't simply leave. We had a deal."

"Apparently she didn't take the deal too seriously." He sighed heavily. "I have patients that I visit, a practice that I run, and rounds at the hospital. I don't have time to babysit. He needs monitoring until he's strong enough to go wherever the hell he came from." He stood straighter. "I can't do it."

Winston glared at him, his jaw clenched. He started to tell Clem just what he could and couldn't do, but knew it would be fruitless. "Isn't there someone you could get in the meantime? Someone from the hospital or the clinic?"

"No one that I would trust enough not to ask questions. Gunshots have to be reported to the police. If anyone ever found out, I'd lose my license to practice."

Winston lowered his head for a moment, trying to think. Clem owed him. If it were not for Winston's intervention, Clem would be peddling coconuts in the market. He'd turned to drink five years ago after his wife was killed in a horrific car accident. Winston had taken him in, sobered him up, and even financed his medical office to get him back on his feet. Winston knew that Clem took plenty of money under the table, undercutting the insurance companies. He'd always looked the other way, and Clem knew it. If he chose to, he could make a few calls and Clem's career would be over. The doctor knew that, too, which proved to Winston that Clem was willing to risk Winston's wrath rather than keep this man under his roof.

"All right, then. He can stay at the guesthouse. If you swear to me that you will continue to check on him until we can get him on his way. I don't want him dying on me either."

"Fine." Clem let out a breath of relief. "I gave him a mild sedative for the trip."

"Come on, then. Let's move him as quickly and quietly as possible."

They hustled out of the house and made their way down the small incline toward the guesthouse.

Clem approached the car first and opened the back door. He jerked back and spun toward Winston. "He's gone."

Winston pushed him out of the way and looked inside. The only indication that someone had been in the backseat was a blanket that had been tossed to the floor.

"What the bloody hell . . ." Winston stepped away and turned in a slow circle, searching in the dark for any sign of Vincent. He stopped, pressed his lips together in concentration.

"Perhaps our mystery man has solved our problem for us," Clem offered.

Winston snapped him a look. He flicked his brows. "Perhaps," he said in a distant voice. "Perhaps."

WHATEVER THE DOCTOR had stuck in his arm definitely took the edge off the pain in his side, but Vincent's head felt as if he were submerged in water. His limbs felt like bricks attached to his joints. He'd feigned sleep after the doctor had given him the shot. Perhaps the good doc shouldn't have been muttering to himself about what he'd planned to do, thinking that Vincent was asleep.

As soon as he was sure the doctor was gone and out of sight, he'd gotten out of the car and over to the front gate, pressed the button, and simply let himself out. So much for security. Hard to get in, easy to get out.

Vincent inched along the darkened paths, staying close to the tree lines until he found the main road. He kept looking behind him, expecting headlights to run up on him at any minute. They never did. He stood for a moment in the center of the road, trying to get his bearings. He really hadn't been on the island long enough to know his way around. He needed to get back to his motel, collect his things, and then find Tess.

After walking for about fifteen minutes, he heard the sound of a car approaching on the gravel road. He stopped and stepped up on the grass.

The car slowed and then stopped in front of him. Music was coming from inside. The window rolled down, and a stunning young woman with an equally stunning friend in the passenger seat were inside.

"You look lost," the woman in the passenger seat said.

"Uh, my car broke down. I'm trying to get back to the Cove Motel."

"You're a long way from the Cove." She turned to the driver and said something he couldn't hear. She turned back to Vincent. "Hop in. We can drop you off."

"Thanks." He opened the back door and got in. "I really appreciate this," he said, wincing just a bit.

"No problem. You're definitely a tourist," the driver said, looking at him through the rearview mirror.

"Yes, just visiting."

"Business or pleasure?"

"Business."

"What kind of business?" the woman in the passenger seat asked.

"Real estate."

"My name is Angelique," the driver said.

"Trinity," the second woman said.

"Vincent."

"So how long do you plan to stay in Aruba?" Angelique asked.

"Until my business is finished."

"No time for a bit of fun while you're here?" Trinity questioned.

Vincent chuckled lightly. *Professionals.* "Not sure how much time I'll have, but I'll keep you ladies in mind."

Trinity opened her purse, took out a card, and handed it to him over the backseat. "Just in case," she said.

Vincent took the card and tucked it into the pocket of the shirt that the doctor must have put on him. He was thankful for the darkness; he must look a mess. But at least his clothes were clean.

"There's a party next weekend. If you're still in town, maybe you'd like to stop by. Plenty of good food, conversation and *contacts,*" Angelique said.

"No promises."

"In case you decide, it's at the Villa Alexandria. Friday. Things will get started around eight."

"Are you ladies throwing this party?"

"No. We're . . . more like . . . hostesses," Trinity said.

Vincent's thoughts began to race. Two beautiful "professional" women, playing hostess at the villa. He'd heard of the place, set off in the hills, overlooking the beach. It was touted as one of the most lavish locations in all of Aruba. Just the kind of place Tess would secure for her business. He had no idea that was the location he was calling when he'd finally tracked her to Aruba. He'd paid one of the local police officers a pretty penny to get him a number.

"There's your motel up ahead," Angelique said. She turned slightly on the road and headed toward the motel. They came to a stop.

"Thank you very much, ladies. It was a pleasure."

"Hope to see you on Friday," Trinity said.

Vincent smiled at both of them. "As I said, no promises. My . . . business may be finished by then."

He opened the door. "Thanks again." He got out and walked toward the front door.

They waited for a moment before pulling off and disappearing into the night.

Vincent stopped at the front door and turned to where the car had been. He looked toward the hills and could just make out the lights that must be coming from the villa. He smiled.

Tess, it was only a matter of time. He turned and went inside.

"Ah, Mr. Vincent, we were worried about you," the hotel clerk said when he walked through the doors of the family-owned business.

"No need to worry." He approached the desk. "I seemed to have lost my key, however."

"Not a problem." He turned behind him and located a spare key on the board then handed it to Vincent. "Do you need anything brought to your room, sir?"

"Is the kitchen still open? I'm starving."

"We can send a small plate. We served flying fish tonight." The clerk grinned with pride.

Vincent nodded. "Sounds fine."

"I'll send it right up."

Vincent walked down the short hallway, turned right, and entered his room at the end of the hall.

He opened the door and was relieved to find it the way he left it.

With much effort he gingerly stripped off his shirt and was pleased to see that he hadn't busted open his stitches again. He was going to have to make a stop at a pharmacy to get some extra bandages and some antibiotic ointment, but he figured he could make it through the night. This wasn't his first gunshot wound, and based on the way he was feeling he was sure he was out of the woods and free of any infections.

He sat down on the bed, running the events of the evening through his head. The women he'd met on the road were certainly two of Tess's "girls." He was sure of it. And she was running her business—or at least recruiting her clientcle—at the villa.

But his instincts, years of investigating experience, and knowledge of Tess all led him to believe that she hadn't returned to the villa. She'd figure that if he'd found her phone number, he would easily track her back there.

So if not there, then where? *Where are you, Tess? And how long do you plan to run before I catch you   and I will catch you.*

He fished in his pants pocket and took out his cell phone. Thankfully, the good doctor had seen fit to make sure he'd kept it. The one thing that was missing, though, was his gun. He'd have to get another one—soon. He had no intention of being ambushed again.

Ten

TESS HAD SPENT the latter part of the day in town, picking up items that she would need: several changes of clothes, undergarments, toiletries, shoes, and makeup. She'd even gone so far as to stop in a local wig shop and select a new "hairdo." With her packages in tow, she checked into the Surf Resort, a small but well-maintained place off the beaten path. It was just far enough out of the way to keep her from the public eye, but close enough for her to do what was needed.

She'd opted to keep the car and had spent the better part of the morning washing down the backseat. At least if she wanted to dump it, there would be no telltale bloodstains to worry about. She'd rented it for a month, but she had no intention of being around that long.

Her room was far from what she was used to, but a damn sight better than that dump of a place she'd had to hide out in back in Brooklyn.

She'd been on the run then, too. She'd had to shut down her businesses—all three locations—send off her ladies, and then find a place to lie low. Her inside information advised her that she would be raided in a matter of days or hours and the person behind it all was her very own sister—Assistant District Attorney Tracy Alexander. Tracy had no idea that the woman she relentlessly hunted was her own sister. At least not until the end.

By the time she'd gotten that last phone call from Tracy, it was too late. Too late to stop the plan that she'd put into motion. First Tracy, then Trust, then Troy. They were all gone. Life was supposed to be good now—better than good. She, Kim, and Nikki had freed themselves of the albatrosses that hung around their necks. Yet, here she was: on the run once again.

She tossed her packages onto the bed and went to open a window. She'd grown to like the natural coolness of the tropical evenings as opposed to turning on the air-conditioning. Go figure. She stood in front of the open window for a few moments, the sheer curtains blowing gently in the light breeze. The more things changed, the more they stayed the same, she thought. She'd gone halfway around the world to get away from the one man who could bring her down only to have him on her heels once again.

But the question that continued to plague her was how had Vincent found her? She was more than certain that she'd covered her tracks. How had he done it? A better question was, why didn't she kill him when she had the chance?

She was too tired to think about it now. She turned away from the window and began unpacking her belongings. She wasn't too sure how long she planned to stay, but in the meantime she wanted to be comfortable and she still had loose ends to tie up.

After a long hot shower, she ordered room service while contemplating what she had to do next. This had to go off without a hitch.

She pushed her tray aside and reached for her cell phone. After punching in the number, she waited.

Charrie picked up on the second ring. "Tess," she said in a hushed voice. "Where are you? Are you all right?"

"Where I am doesn't matter, and I'm fine. But, we need to talk. I'm going to make this brief." She took a breath. "I have to leave Aruba."

"What!"

"Just listen. I have to leave in order to protect the business and everyone connected to it. You know where all the information is for the bank accounts; you know the escape plan and the rules of the house."

"Why are you doing this, Tess? Everything is fine here. It's not like New York."

"Sometimes your past has a way of following you."

"What do you mean?"

"It doesn't matter."

"Did . . . you take care of what you left here to do the other night?"

"That's why I have to leave."

"What do I tell everyone?"

"Business as usual. I had to go out of town for an indeterminate amount of time. You are running the business. You need to work Kim and Nikki into the operations. I promised them, and I don't break my promises. You know everyone that I know. They trust you as they would trust me. You'll be fine."

"Tell me, honestly. How long will you be gone?"

"I don't know." She waited a beat. "There are some things I need you to do for me."

"Anything."

"This is what I need . . ."

After speaking with Tess, Charrie slowly hung up the phone. So this was it. She didn't know what to do with her feelings. This was the opportunity she'd worked so long to achieve. Now it was unceremoniously dumped in her lap. But she was ready. She'd been grooming for this for years.

She hooked her cell phone onto the belt clip on her white linen slacks and walked out of the kitchen.

Charrie wandered over to the pool area and surveyed the few folks lounging around. Several of their new clients were being looked after by the ladies. She smiled and walked over to one of the lounge chairs near the bar. She stretched out, relaxing in her new position as head bitch in charge, and closed her eyes.

She'd been only eighteen when she met Tess. They'd both lived in D.C. at the time. She was working part-time at the local spa in Georgetown as a personal trainer. The moment she set eyes on Tess, she knew the woman was someone special, someone she would like to emulate. There was an air about her, a control and a sensuality that was right there on the surface but not overpowering. The men in the coed spa virtually stopped what they were doing to watch her walk by.

Tess McDonald was not what would be considered beautiful. In truth, she was rather ordinary to look at, but there was a charisma about her—the way she walked, moved her body, her personal style, and self-assurance—that created the beautiful package.

The manager of the spa had brought Tess over to meet Charrie. "Ms. McDonald, this is our personal trainer, Charrie Lewis."

Charrie smiled. "I would shake your hand, but I'm kinda sweaty."

"I appreciate that."

"Ms. McDonald is interested in working with you a couple of days per week. Why don't you tell her about your training regime." He nodded toward Tess. "Once you're done, come see me in the office."

"Thank you." She turned back to Charrie, looked her over from head to toe. Charrie felt herself blush. "You look like you're in good shape."

"I try. Can't very well market a product if you can't represent it."

The corner of Tess's mouth curved. "I like how you think." She began to walk around the facility, forcing Charrie to follow her.

"How long have you been working here?"

"About six months. It's helps pay for school."

"Really. You're a student?"

"Yes. I'm a Communications major."

Tess nodded and continued strolling. "With school and work, you must not have much time for your family."

"I don't have any family."

Tess stopped and turned behind her. She frowned. "No family?"

"My parents—my adoptive parents—were killed in a house fire two years ago. I went to a group home until I aged out at eighteen."

"You seem to be doing well for yourself."

Charrie shrugged then lowered her gaze, wondering why she'd confessed all that to a perfect stranger. "I get by."

Tess folded her arms. "I have a proposition for you, one that will pay you three times as much as you make here *and* pay for your education."

Charrie's eyes widened in surprise and apprehension. Who was this woman? She looked quickly around. "What do you mean?"

Tess went into her purse and handed her a card. "Call me." Charrie took the card. "Now, let's go tell that boss of yours that he can sign me up. For now." She walked ahead of Charrie to the office.

That's how it began. She started off as Tess's personal trainer by day, and personal assistant by night and on her days off. Her duties were simple at first: answer phones and make appointments. Over time, Tess began to trust her with more responsibility, letting her meet some of the ladies and accompany them on doctor visits and shopping trips. Tess never actually came out and said what it was that she did, but Charrie knew. It wasn't the modeling agency it claimed to be.

The sound of familiar voices behind her pulled her away from her musings.

"He was kind of cute," Angelique was saying. "In that rugged kind of way."

"I'd sure like to clean him up and take him out," Trinity said with a giggle.

"Maybe he'll come to the party on Friday and we can see for ourselves."

"What did he say his name was again? Vernon?"

"Vincent."

Charrie's ears perked up.

"Good thing he wasn't some kind of psycho. But he looked too yummy."

"Yeah, we took a major chance picking up a stranger on the road."

Charrie sat up, and then she stood. She faced the ladies.

Angelique and Trinity jumped in surprise.

"Interesting conversation you were having. Would you mind coming with me." The women looked at each other. "It wasn't a question," Charrie said before turning and walking toward the house.

Trinity and Angelique meekly followed Charrie back inside the house.

Charrie went directly into the room that had been established as the lounge. She didn't bother to sit. "Shut the door."

Angelique did.

Charrie turned toward them, her arms tightly folded. "First, don't attempt to insult my intelligence by telling me that I didn't hear you say that you picked up some strange man on the road and invited him here." The words shot out like bullets, all direct hits. She glared from one to the other.

"Charrie, we can—"

"Who is he?"

"He said his name was Vincent."

"Who is he?" she repeated.

"He's here on business. Not long."

"He's not even sure if he'll be here long enough to come to the party," Trinity said, her expression clearly terrified.

Charrie's voice dropped to a chilling monotone. "When you were asked to become a part of this organization, you were advised of the rules. You were told in no uncertain terms that all of our clients were to be fully screened by either myself or Tess. That under *no* circumstances was anyone *ever* to be invited here without our knowledge and permission." Her smile was tight and mean. "Yet, both of you had no problem breaking a major rule. A rule that keeps us all safe. You jeopardized everything with your stupidity."

"It will never happen again. Never," Angelique pleaded.

Charrie turned away, walked behind the desk, and sat down. She opened the center drawer and took out a key, then opened the bottom drawer on the right.

After several moments, she sat up with two envelopes in her hand. She extended them toward Trinity and Angelique.

"Inside is your severance pay, along with your ticket back home." She almost laughed at the stunned looks on their faces. "We're always prepared. There's a ticket and a good-bye pack for everyone." She stood and pushed the drawer closed. "I'll expect you to be off the premises in fifteen minutes. I will have a car take you to the airport. Those are open tickets. Be on the next flight."

"Charrie, please," Trinity begged. "I can't go back home. I can't."

"You should have thought of that before you fucked up. There's enough money in there to set you up once you get back home. Move where you want. Anywhere but New York or here. If I find out, and I will . . . Let's just leave it at that."

Angelique had tears in her eyes. She took the envelope. "I'm sorry," she murmured. Charrie didn't respond.

Trinity took her envelope without a word and stormed out.

"I'll be holding you both to the confidentiality agreement that you signed," she called out to their departing backs.

After they'd left, Charrie slowly sat down. She was so much like them when she'd first started, eager and anxious. Young, beautiful, and raw. That was ten years ago. She'd changed, matured. She understood that to stay in business—any business—you often had to make the hard decisions, get rid of people, hurt feelings.

She had power over people's lives she suddenly realized, and the surge of that knowledge heated her from the inside. Is this how Tess felt as she moved all her players around on her master chessboard? She'd idolized Tess, from day one. All she dreamed about was being like her. That is, until she found out the truth.

eleven

TESS WAS RELAXING on the bed, mindlessly surfing through the channels on the television. The bedside phone rang. She reached for it.

"Yes?"

"Ms. Moore, you have a guest."

"Thanks. Send her over." She hung up. Her extra ID came in handy, she thought while hanging up the phone. She put on her robe and tied the belt just as the knock came.

"Come in." She kissed Charrie's cheek and let her into the room. "You find everything?"

"Yes." She put the small travel bag on the chair near the bed.

"Let's sit on the terrace." She opened the sliding glass doors and stepped outside. Charrie followed. Tess sat down on one of the lawn chairs. "Thanks for doing this."

"Can't you tell me how long you'll be gone?"

"I don't know. But it's for the best. Believe that."

"Where are you going—can you tell me that at least?"

"I'll be in touch when I can." She reached out and took Charrie's hand. "You'll be fine. Everything is in place."

"This has to do with that man, doesn't it?"

Tess looked away for an instant. "Something like that."

"You've never let a man get in the way of business." She swallowed. "Come between us . . . things."

"And no man is coming between things now," she said, jabbing her finger in the air.

Charrie stared at her. A slow fury began to brew inside her. *I'll always be here for you, Charrie.* She heard the words now as clearly as she had years ago when she'd cried in Tess's arms about feeling so alone in the world. Tess promised always to be there for her. Always. She'd lied.

Charrie lifted her chin. "I'll take care of everything."

"I know. You have *skills,* girl." Tess smiled.

"When are you leaving?"

"In the morning."

Charrie swallowed and nodded her head. "So this is it, huh?"

"Yeah. For now."

She was lying. She'd never come back. "Well, I guess I should go."

Tess stood up. They faced each other.

Charrie turned and walked slowly toward the door. She opened it and then turned back to Tess. "Safe travels," she said softly.

"Thanks," Tess whispered.

Charrie walked out. Tess stood in the doorway until Charrie

turned down the corridor and was gone. She closed the door and drew in a long breath.

Step one.

CHARRIE DROVE BLINDLY back to the villa. Her emotions ran the gamut from elation to fear, anger, and joy to betrayal. Tears clouded her vision.

"I did everything for you, Tess!" she screamed, slamming her fist onto the steering wheel. *I lived and breathed for you, until I found out who you really were.*

She sped along the dark roads, seeing images of the rainy night that Tess had left the villa in the middle of the party. *There were two of them lit by the moonlight. Her intention had been to rid herself of Tess McDonald once and for all. But at the last second . . .*

The villa loomed ahead. Charrie sniffed hard and swiped at her eyes.

She went straight to her bedroom, shut and locked her door. For several moments she paced the floor, chewing on her thumbnail. She picked up the phone and dialed a New York number; then she paid a visit to Kim and Nikki.

They were out on the back deck. She schooled her expression and approached. "Ladies, we need to talk."

Nikki turned from the barstool, and Kim looked up from reading her magazine.

"About what?" Nikki practically sneered.

Charrie lifted her brow and lowered her voice. "About things that shouldn't be heard by others." She challenged Nikki with her own glare.

Kim tossed aside her magazine. "Where do you want to talk?"

"In the office."

"Fine," Nikki mumbled.

They followed Charrie back into the house, intermittently flashing each other questioning looks.

Charrie opened the door to the room that served as the office and stepped inside. "Please, have a seat."

Kim and Nikki sat down in two of the rattan armchairs. Nikki crossed her legs.

"I probably should have told you both this before."

"Before what?" Nikki asked, barely hiding her contempt.

"Before now," Charrie said, cool and controlled. She drew in a breath, gazed at them as if they were all the best of friends sharing a secret.

"I don't know all the details," she began, "but the night of the party, Tess got a call. I shouldn't have listened, but when I picked up the extension . . ." She looked mildly shamefaced. "Anyway, she was talking to Vincent." She looked at them both, hoping to see some sort of recognition on their faces. "She mentioned your names and said something like *they know everything that happened.*"

Nikki stiffened in her seat. Kim remained impassive, the only sign that she was paying attention was the slight flush in her cheeks.

"Whatever she's planning, he's in it with her."

"Planning?" Kim asked.

"Isn't it obvious? She's planning to shut you both up about whatever it is between you. She met with him that night. And, as we all know, she hasn't been back, won't return calls." Her eyes darted from one to the other.

"What gave you your attack of conscience?" Kim asked.

"I know what it's like to be in a new place, with high expectations, being uncertain and depending on someone to make everything right." She stood in front of the desk and rested her butt on the edge. "I know Tess. Tess is manipulative and Tess is ruthless. That's why she is as good as she is. She has no qualms about getting people out of her way." She held up her hands. "I don't know what went down with you and her, but whatever it is, as far as Tess is concerned, it's unfinished business that needs to be tied up."

Kim pushed up from her seat. "Thanks for the information."

Nikki stared at her for a minute. She cocked her head to the side. "How do we know that you aren't behind Tess's disappearance and now want us out of the way so that you can do the damn thing on your own?"

"You don't. You have no reason to trust me. But the facts speak for themselves. Do with them as you wish."

"We will," Nikki said as she stood up. She turned and stalked out.

"If what you're saying is true, we are in danger, aren't we?" Kim asked.

Charrie slowly nodded her head.

Kim's right fist clenched and unclenched. She walked out.

Charrie leaned back against the edge of the desk and smiled.

TWELVE

VINCENT HAD TAPED a strip of plastic around his midsection to protect the bandage from water. He desperately needed a hot, steaming bath but opted for a shower instead.

Feeling almost human again, he emerged from the bathroom just as his food was being delivered by the hotel owner's teenage son.

"Thanks a lot, Sam. It smells delicious." He took the tray.

"It's my mother's specialty. Enjoy your meal and your evening."

Vincent felt light-headed from the tantalizing aroma of his dinner. He couldn't remember the last time he'd eaten. He took the tray to his night table and sat on the edge of the bed, ready to dig in, just as his cell phone rang.

"Shit." He tossed his napkin aside and snatched up the phone, peering at the number in the lighted display. He frowned. It could only mean trouble. He depressed the handset icon.

"Yes?"

"How are things in sunny Aruba?"

"I won't be sending postcards."

The caller chuckled. "I just thought you should know, if you don't already, that Tess is planning to leave, in a hurry."

Vincent was paying attention now. He kept his voice even. "How do you know that?"

"I told you I have my sources."

"You knew I was coming here to look for Tess."

"I knew you couldn't resist, once you got a whiff of where she was. Don't make this personal. This is business."

"You think you're still pulling my strings, Avery?"

"I wouldn't go that far, but I do know when a man will fly a few miles for a piece of ass like Tess McDonald."

"I'm not bringing her in." Why had he said that?

"Better you than one of us, Vinny."

"Forget it."

Avery snickered. "Was it that good? Got your mind and your morals all twisted over some snatch! Come on, Vincent. Think."

"I gotta go, Avery. Thanks for the call. If I have anything to do with it, we won't be speaking again."

"You're going to throw your career down the toilet? The Bureau doesn't forget shit like this. You'll shoot right up to the top of their list."

"Good-bye, Avery."

Vincent ran his hand over his face. Tess leaving? If Avery already knew, then she could be on her way by now. And now that he'd cut his ties, dug his own hole, and put a noose around his neck, he was as much on the run as Tess was. He had to find her before someone else did—even if she had tried to kill him.

Suddenly he was no longer hungry. He took a couple of bites, then pushed the plate aside. A bit achy, he stood and went to the closet for a change of clothes.

Once dressed, he headed out to the front desk.

The clerk looked up from reading a magazine and smiled. "How was your meal?"

"Great. Listen, is there any way I can get a car?"

The clerk frowned in concentration. "Most of our guests come with their own or rent them at the airport." He looked at Vincent and wagged his finger. "I remember you had a car when you arrived."

"Yes, I did. It broke down."

"Oh, I'm sorry." He paused a moment. "I suppose I can loan you my car. How long will you be gone?"

"A couple of hours at best."

He reached into his pants pocket and pulled out a set of car keys. "It's the blue Toyota out back."

"Thanks, Mr. Hampton. I'll be real careful. Promise." He took the keys, started to leave, but stopped. "Uh, one more thing, do you have a map?"

"Certainly." He gave Vincent a map from beneath the desk. "And here is a guide of all the sights." He took out a brochure from the holder on the front desk.

Vincent saluted with the map and brochure. "Thanks." He walked out back as quickly as he could and located the car in the small lot.

He was working on pure adrenaline and instinct at this point. He was certain Tess wasn't at the villa, but he had a good idea that Avery's informant was. Maybe the snitch would be willing to share some information with him as well.

After a few wrong turns, he found the road that led to the villa. He pulled up on the grounds and strolled to the front door. There was no bell, but rather, a knocker. He used it and waited.

"Yes, may I help you?" asked a stunning young woman.

"Yes, I'm looking for Tess. I'm an old friend. She told me to stop by when I got into town."

"I'm sorry. Tess had some business to take care of. She had to go away."

Vincent's expression collapsed in disappointment. "Wow. Do you have any idea when she'll be back?"

"No, I don't. But I'd be happy to get a message to her when I hear from her."

"Tell her that Vincent stopped by."

Charrie's heart knocked in her chest. *Vincent. This is him, up close?* She swallowed. "Uh, why don't you leave me your number?"

"Your name?"

"Charrie."

He flashed all his teeth. "So we finally meet. Tess has told me so much about you."

"She has?" she asked, both complimented and perplexed by the news. She had no idea Tess spoke about her to anyone outside "the family." "I wish I could say the same."

Vincent shrugged. "Go figure. About that number . . ."

"Yes. Do you have a card?"

He patted his empty pockets. "No. But if you have a pen and paper, I'll write it down for you."

Charrie pressed her lips together. She needed to get him out of there as quickly as possible. The last thing she needed was for Kim or Nikki to walk up on her and discover that this was "the" Vincent. "Just a moment. Wait right here." She walked to the foyer and quickly pulled open the top drawer of the antique desk, retrieving a pad and pen. Her hands were shaking. She returned to the door and practically shoved the items at Vincent.

"I was invited to your party next week."

"Oh, the party." She laughed lightly. "We're not sure if we're still having it. Especially with Tess gone."

"That's too bad." He handed her the pen and pad. "If you change your mind, give me a call." He grinned and ran his gaze up and down her body.

Charrie forced a tight smile. "Thanks for stopping by. As soon as I hear from Tess, I'll make sure to give her your number."

"Thanks a lot, Charrie. It was nice to meet you."

She didn't comment.

Vincent returned to his car and drove away.

Charrie was shaking all over. Fool! She'd had the opportunity, and she'd let it go, and now her mistake in judgment was back to haunt her. She couldn't risk having him return and Kim and Nicole meeting him. That was not an option.

What would Tess do? Think. Think. She hurried to her bedroom and shut the door. She dialed Tess on her cell phone. Hopefully she was still somewhere in reach.

Tess's phone rang until the voice mail came on. Charrie left an innocuous message, simply asking that Tess call her back.

Moments later, her cell phone rang.

"Charrie, it's Tess."

"You had a visitor."

"What? Who?"

"He said his name was Vincent." She heard Tess's short intake of breath.

"Vincent was there?" *But I left him at the doctor's place.* "Are you sure he said his name was Vincent?"

"That's what he said. Tall, dark, extremely sexy. A body to dream about. Sound familiar?"

Tess didn't respond.

"Anyway, he left a message. He said you told him to stop by."

He was lying. He was fishing for information. "What did you tell him?"

"I said you had to leave on business and I wasn't sure when you would be back."

"Good."

"Are you planning to see him before you leave?"

"No."

"Tess. Who is he really?"

"An old acquaintance."

"If he's the reason you're leaving—"

"I'm not going to discuss this with you, Charrie," Tess said, her tone strident. "End of story."

"Fine. He left a number. Do you want it?"

"Give it to me." She programmed the number into her cell phone. "Thanks. I'll be in touch." She disconnected the call.

Sometimes the best way to get rid of your enemies is to pit them against each other. Charrie put the phone down and went to see what was for dinner.

TESS STARED at the number she'd just programmed into her phone. Why had he gone there? She was pretty sure he knew she wouldn't be at the villa. He knew she'd find out about his visit.

He wanted her to know. He was hunting her. But she had no intention of being a deer trapped in the headlights.

She dialed Winston. "I need to see you."

"Do you have any idea the trouble you've caused?" he said in a harsh whisper. "That friend of yours is gone."

"I know. That's what I want to talk to you about. Can you meet me?"

"No. I can't get away. Meet me at the guesthouse. I'll come over about eleven. My guests will be gone by then."

"Thank you, Winston. I swear to you, I will explain everything when I see you. I owe you that."

He cleared his throat. "Eleven."

Tess disconnected the call. It was a little after nine. She had more than an hour to kill before she would drive over to Winston's estate.

She arrived at the guesthouse about ten forty-five and waited. So much had gone wrong so quickly, she thought as she turned off the engine. All her planning was for nothing. It was all falling apart. The words of her friend Dr. Annette Hutchinson drifted to mind: *Maybe it's time you give this life up.*

Annette was her private gynecologist. But more than that, Annette had been her friend. One of the only ones she had that she trusted with her secret life. All Tess's girls had been patients of Annette's over the years. Tess did most of her recruiting right in Annette's waiting room. It was where she'd discovered Kim and Nicole.

She had refused Annette's plea to give up the life.

Please Netti, don't lecture me. I know where you're heading. . . . It may not be an honorable profession I'm in, but I never hurt anyone, I never stole, cheated, or lied. All I've done is use what I was born with to

*make men happy—and myself a wealthy woman. I've traveled and met
some of the most incredible people. I simply make men pay for what other
women give away willingly. And someone thinks they have the right to
take that away from me! Why? Because I've committed some great sin?*

*For God's sake, Tess, let it go. You've had a good run. Walk away
while you still can.*

*I don't think so. . . . Thank you for being my friend, Nettie . . . and
don't worry, I'll be fine.*

She should have listened, taken heed and cut her losses before
the toll became so great. She wasn't fine. For all that she thought
she would achieve and acquire, what she'd lost overshadowed
everything. What's more, if she turned herself in or, worse, was
caught, it would not only end the life she knew but also suck Kimberly and Nicole along with her. She may be a lot of things, but
disloyal and dishonorable were not among them.

The light tapping on her window startled her. A face peered
into the glass.

She took her purse, phone, and car keys and got out. "Thank
you for meeting me."

Winston put his arm around her shoulder. "Let's get inside."

Anxious and for the first time uncomfortable in Winston's
presence, she walked in and sat down, holding her purse tightly in
her lap.

"I don't think I've ever seen you not cool and in control, Tess,"
Winston commented. He went to the bar. "Can I fix you a drink?"

She waved her hand. "No. Thanks."

Winston took his time fixing a snifter of brandy and then sat
opposite her. "I'm listening."

She looked directly at him. "First, you can't know how sorry I
am about all this."

He shrugged it off. "No apologies needed. I know you well enough to know that you wouldn't intentionally set out to screw me. And not in the biblical sense." That drew a short smile from her.

"When did he leave?"

Winston took a sip of his drink. "From what Clem told me, when he returned, your friend was passed out on the floor. He closed up a couple of busted stitches, bandaged him up, and gave him a mild sedative, then brought him here."

"Here? I don't understand."

"The why is not important. The fact is, Clem drove over here with him in the backseat. He came up to the main house to get me. When we returned to the car, he was gone."

Tess heaved a sigh.

"Who is this man, that you would be willing to risk so much and involve so many people?"

Tess clasped and unclasped her hand, finally entwining her fingers before she spoke. "A little more than a year ago, I got an anonymous tip that my establishment in Manhattan was going to be raided in a major vice bust, precipitated by none other than my dear sister, ADA Tracy Alexander."

His eyes widened, but he didn't interrupt. He took a long swallow of his drink.

"Of course, I always had an escape plan in the event something like that would ever happen. I put it into action and dismantled the business. Paid everyone off, and I lay low in Brooklyn for a while until things blew over. It was while I was staying in Brooklyn that I met Vincent."

Winston noted the faraway look in her eyes and the way her

voice softened when she said his name. This Vincent was more than another a quick fuck for Tess. He knew that expression; she'd had it for him once upon a time. He suddenly resented this Vincent who had made such an indelible impression on Tess McDonald that she was willing to sacrifice so much to protect him.

"We got involved," she was saying, drawing Winston back to her story. "And one night, I found out that he was working undercover in order to take me down."

Winston lowered his glass to the table. "Tess . . . I'm sorry."

A sad smile flickered around her mouth. "It was all my fault, really. I knew better than to get involved with anyone, to let my emotions do my thinking for me." She looked across at him. "It had already happened once."

Winston looked away. He knew what he'd left behind when he left Tess, but he'd had no choice. None. Did he regret his decision? It depended on the day.

"Anyway, when I found out, I knew I had to get away—far away and for good. Somewhere that I couldn't be found and no one would care who I had been in the past . . . the elusive Madame X who'd built an enterprise on the sale of sex. Who had politicians, businessmen, and police chiefs as bedmates and confidants and even a wavering clergyman once or twice." She looked at him and winked. "Once I'd settled everything, I came here, where I thought I'd be safe, where I knew I had a friend."

"And he followed you?"

"Yes. I have no idea how he could possibly have known where I was. I didn't even travel under my own name."

"Maybe you're not as good as you think you are."

She shot him a look. "Oh, I am. That's not it. I know it."

He reached for his snifter and leaned back against the plush cushions of the couch. "Sometimes we unconsciously do things because there is a buried part of us that wants the very thing we protest about to actually happen."

"What are you talking about?"

"Maybe there was a part of you that wanted Vincent to find you. And that part of you did leave a stone unturned to lead him to you."

Tess vehemently shook her head. "No. Never. There was too much at stake. I wouldn't do that. Not even for Vincent." She stared right at him.

"Then if you're so certain you didn't leave a trail behind that he could follow, how did he find you?"

"I wish I knew. All I do know is that out of the blue I get a call from him telling me to meet him. I do, but before we could talk, he got shot."

"You mean you shot him."

She swallowed. "That was my intention." She nodded her head, thinking back to that night and the fateful decision she'd made. "I was going to shoot him, stop him for good. But . . . before I did, someone else did it for me."

"You didn't shoot him?"

"No. I swear to you I didn't."

"Then who did?"

"That's the question I've been battling for days, racking my brain trying to think who could have done it. I don't think he was here long enough to build any gripes with someone who'd want to shoot him to settle it. I could be wrong."

"How did he know where to find you? You said he called you?"

"I was careful. No one knew where I was heading when I came here."

"Yet, he knew just where to call. Maybe one of your 'guests'?"

"At this point, anything is possible."

"And maybe that same person regretted giving out the information and decided to shut him up to avoid your wrath if you ever found out."

They were both silent for a minute.

"But, even if that were true—and it's a stretch—that still doesn't explain how he knew that you were here in Aruba. Someone knew and someone told. Someone close to you."

She looked at him. "No," she whispered. Her mind wouldn't accept what it was conjuring up. She shook the thought away.

"What are you going to do? It's apparent that this Vincent is relentless."

"I've begun sprinkling bread crumbs leading him away from here. That's all I can tell you."

"I can't have any of this lead back to me—ever. You know I'd do anything for you—but I won't risk my career and become embroiled in a scandal."

"I know. I know all about your career. You wouldn't risk it back then when you were barely a name over here. I know you won't risk it now."

"That's not fair, and you know it. I was married, for God's sake. I had a political future ahead of me. I'm prime minister now. Do you think any of that would have happened—?"

She held up her hand to cut him off. "No need to explain. I understand. I just don't have to like it." She smiled and meant it.

The tight line between Winston's brow slowly began to ease.

"If you hadn't been married, do you think it would have worked with us?"

"Ah, Tess," he said on a breath of memory. "How many nights did I lie awake thinking of you even as my wife slept next to me? But I couldn't indulge myself in fantasies. I was so unlike you. Where you were uninhibited, I was bound by rules and obligations. So much was expected of me, and I'd been raised never to disappoint.

"I thought of you often. And when Marissa died, I allowed myself to truly wonder how it could have been between us. I never really loved Marissa. I respected her. Our marriage was arranged since we were kids. It was purely about two families joining in the name of power and success. Marissa had her life, and I had mine. We kept it discreet, but we would never have divorced."

"You never had children?"

"No. Marissa couldn't have kids. What an ironic twist of fate. Over time, it made her bitter and cold. Our union was to spawn a new dynasty in Aruba, but my family name will end with me." He gave a sad smile of acceptance.

"I'm sorry."

"Water under the bridge, my dear."

She pushed up from her seat. "I really should go."

"Where are you staying?"

"It's best that you don't know." She started for the door.

"Even if they pull out my fingernails, I'll only give them my name and rank."

Tess chuckled. "Thank you, Winston, for everything. I mean that."

He looked down into her upturned face. "I know." He touched

her chin with his forefinger and looked deep into her eyes. His voice suddenly took on a harsh edge. "I can make sure he never finds you again." His meaning was clear.

Tess's chest constricted. "I'll handle it."

His gaze held her for a moment. "Be safe. My life would be so much more meaningful if I knew I'd see you again—sometime."

"I loved you once," she said in a soft response and walked out.

Winston drew in a long breath and shoved his hands in his pockets. *So did I, Tess. So did I.*

Tess got into her car and slowly pulled away. Her eyes burned with unshed tears. Winston had a child out there somewhere. Raised by people she'd never known.

The day she gave birth to her baby should have been the happiest day of her life. But she'd never felt more alone.

"Are you sure you don't want to hold your baby once before . . . ?" the nurse had asked.

Tess turned on her side away from the nurse holding a bundle wrapped in white.

"No."

"Do you want know what you had?"

"No."

The nurse walked out. That was as close as she'd ever come to seeing the child of Winston's that she'd carried for nine months.

She'd signed adoption papers months earlier. Her stipulations had been clear: once the baby was born, she didn't want to see it or know its sex. She knew that if she did, she'd never be able to go through with the adoption. After all, what kind of mother would she be? She was well on her way to being a very successful escort. The money was good, and it would only get better. That's all that mattered. She'd seen what happened when she allowed emotion to enter her life. Emotion hurt. Love hurt. If she had neither, she would be fine. And she was. For more than twenty-seven years, she'd been just fine.

Until she'd met Vincent.

THIRTEEN

THE WEATHER FORECAST announced a severe storm warning. The prediction was for a minimum of three to four feet of snow over the next twenty-four to forty-eight hours, with temperatures well below zero. The residents in and around Colorado Springs were told to buckle down. The local supermarkets and hardware stores were packed with shoppers and quickly running out of supplies. The sky was already a cool gray. The air was still and bone cold. Heavy clouds hung ominously over the peaks of the Rocky Mountains.

Tracy went out to do all her shopping and stocking up of supplies the minute the stores were open. Her SUV was loaded with frozen foods, canned goods, juice, eggs, meat, bread, plenty of bottled water (pipes were known to freeze), flashlights, candles, and two electric heaters.

Although the winter had been slightly above inconvenient so far, this was the first major storm of the season.

Tracy unloaded her groceries and put out the ingredients for a big pot of beef stew. She knew that it would last a few days, and she loved the smell of home-cooked soup during chilly winter days.

As she chopped onions, celery, and carrots and listened to the news from the small kitchen radio, her thoughts kept going back to the case she'd been handed. So far, she still couldn't make any connection or arrive at any conclusion as to why these men were killed and how, if at all, the wife and girlfriend were involved.

Maybe now that she would be stuck in the house for the next few days, she'd be able to give it her undivided attention.

Tracy added some seasoning and two capfuls of oil to the boiling water then gently tossed in her chopped vegetables. A mouthwatering aroma soon filled the air. She was humming along to a Luther Vandross number that had come on the radio, when the phone rang.

She wiped her hands on a dish towel and picked up the wall phone next to the china cabinet.

"Hey, babe, it's me."

"Mark. I know you heard the weather report."

"Yes, that's why I'm calling. Do you need anything from outside?"

"Nope. I was a good Girl Scout and went out first thing this morning." She felt a pinch of guilt. It hadn't crossed her mind to call Mark, yet he'd called her.

"Good for you." He chuckled lightly. "Well, if you're up for it, how would you like something warm and cuddly to snuggle up against and watch the snow fall out of those big windows of yours?"

"Is this warm cuddly thing bigger than a bread box?"

"Just a little."

They both laughed.

"I'd love to have you over. I'm pretty sure I have everything we need, but if there's something special you want, bring it along."

"Great. I'll throw a bag together and some old movies. Got any popcorn?"

She thought about it for a minute. "No. Sorry."

"I'll bring some."

She giggled. "Sounds good to me. Hey, would you mind helping me seal some of these windows? I've been getting really bad drafts lately. And I'd hate to wake up with a foot of snow in my house."

"No problem. I have some heavy-duty plastic in the garage. I'll bring that along, too."

"Thanks. Listen, you need to get moving. The wind is starting to kick up, and it's getting darker by the minute." She walked toward the kitchen window and looked skyward. "I see some flakes coming down already."

"I'll be there as soon as I can," he said before they hung up.

Tracy started a pot of rice going and set rolls to baking, for the perfect touch.

While dinner cooked, Tracy sorted and washed a load of linens. In no time, the two-story house was filled with the cozy aromas of simmering stew and fresh laundry.

Tracy walked to the window and peeked out. Since she'd last

looked, a good two to three inches had fallen, and it was still coming down fast and furious.

She let the curtain fall back into place. She certainly hoped that
Mark was more than halfway there. Tracy was actually looking
forward to spending time with him. Although she'd decided to
work on the new case during the storm, she realized that suddenly work wasn't that important anymore. When was the last
time a case hadn't been important to her?

She laughed lightly and with a hint of sadness. How awful was
that? Had that been her life for so many years: work, success, no-
toriety, prosecuting the criminals whether guilty or not? She knew
she'd bent the rules, turned a blind eye on many cases. But her
goal had been to win at any cost, and her quest had been relentless
to the exclusion of everything else, even her marriage to Scott
Alexander.

When she'd married Scott right out of college, she had high
hopes. Although she was going to law school, Scott supported her
ambitions even as he pursued his own career in corporate Amer-
ica. But somewhere along the road, their courses forked and they
went off in different directions.

"I don't know who you are anymore, Tracy," Scott had said to
her over a loveless restaurant dinner.

"I'm the same woman you married five years ago." She took a
sip of her wine and thought about the case waiting for her on her
desk at the office.

"No, you're not. You've turned into this cold machine that's
programmed only for work, and criminals. It's all you talk about,
all you care about."

She put down her glass and shot him a look. "Maybe because
there are some really bad muthafuckers out here, Scott. And I want

to get rid of them so *you* can sleep at night and feel safe on the street."

"Save the world, is that it?"

"One crooked bastard at a time." She lifted her fork then put it back down. "You used to be with me step for step. We were going to conquer the world together. Now . . ." She shook her head and stabbed at her salmon steak.

"Because somewhere along the way, T, you lost your soul. Maybe it got corrupted by all the violence and tragedy that you see every day. I don't know. What I do know is that the person I fell in love with is gone. And she's not coming back." He swallowed.

Tracy grew very still.

"I've filed for divorce."

Tracy twisted her lips as if searching for words. Her chest heaved.

"I want a clean and easy break. I've already gotten a small apartment on the Upper West Side. I can drop you off at home if you want, but that's where I'll be from now on."

Her head began to pound. What the hell was he saying? He was leaving her? His words drifted in and out of her consciousness . . . *pick up my things . . . sell the condo . . . don't want to hurt each other . . . I want the best for you . . . I wish it could have worked.*

She blinked as he was getting up from their table.

"Do you want me to take you home?"

She thought she shook her head, but maybe she'd actually said no, she couldn't be sure.

"Fine." He reached into his wallet and pulled out thirty dollars. "Here's money for a cab, then."

She pushed it back across the table, finally coming to her senses. "I don't need your money, Scott. Thanks for the offer."

Scott drew himself up and buttoned his suit. He didn't take back the money. "Good-bye, Tracy."

Did she hear an echo of sadness, or was it only wishful thinking? When she looked again, Scott was gone and so was her marriage.

With nothing and no one to stop her, Tracy worked until she could barely see. She took on the hardest cases to bring to trial and won decision after decision.

But there was one case that dogged her, taunted her like none other—uncovering the identity of Madame X and bringing down her and her organization.

Tracy laughed sadly and turned to look out the window again. Her zeal had led to an attempt on her life, the discovery that it was her own sister whom she was pursuing, and ultimately having to fake her own death in order to live. And what was it all for—truth, justice, and the American way. What a crock of shit. She shook her head and chuckled at the irony of it all.

She heard the sound of an engine coming to a stop. She hopped up from the couch and hurried to the front door. Not thinking, she opened it and was slammed with a gust of icy cold wind and snow.

"Whoa!" She grabbed her coat from the rack by the door, put it on, and darted outside to help Mark with his bags. The snow was already up to the middle of her calf.

"You should have stayed inside!" he shouted over the wind.

"The two of us will make this faster. Come on."

He draped his duffle bag over his shoulder, handed her a roll of heavy plastic and a tool bag. He grabbed another smaller duffle bag from the backseat and then shut the truck's door.

"That's it."

They ran to the front door and tumbled inside, laughing.

"Wow, for once the weatherman was right," Tracy said, shaking off the snow. She looked down at her jeans. They were soaked almost up to her knees.

"He may even have underestimated. It's really coming down out there. The roads will be totally impassable in another couple of hours."

"It's good you got here when you did." Tracy walked to the kitchen. Mark followed with one of the bags. He deposited it on the counter near the sink.

"I'm the snack man," he joked. "That bag is full of snacks: chips, popcorn, pretzels, and a six-pack of beer."

"That ought to hold us," she teased.

"Something sure smells good."

Tracy went to the stove to check on the stew. "Coming along, coming along." She put the lid back on and turned right into Mark's arms. "No peeking," she said.

"But can't I at least kiss the cook?"

"Of course."

He kissed her long and slow. "Hmmm, I think I'm going to like this snuggling thing. I hope the snow keeps falling until we run out of food or wear each other out, whichever comes first."

She playfully pushed him away. "Go sit down and stay out of trouble."

"Sure." He backed up. "Can I commandeer a drawer to stash my stuff? I hate living out of a bag."

"Yeah. No problem."

They went upstairs, and Tracy made room in one of her drawers for the few of his belongings and gave him hangers for the two fleece shirts he'd brought along and a pair of jeans.

"I've never hung my stuff in a woman's closet before," he said in such a thoughtful tone that it caused Tracy to stop refolding her sweaters and look at him.

"What do you mean?"

"I mean it never mattered enough for me to hang around long enough to do it."

"Oh." She fidgeted with the sweater in her hand. Mark approached.

"It's different with you, Vicky." He searched her eyes. "The more I'm around you, the more I want to be. I think of you all day long, wondering what you're doing, if you're happy, how I can make you happy." He hung his head and sputtered an embarrassed laugh. "Sounds real lame, I know." He lifted his head and looked directly at her. "But it's true."

"I don't know what to say."

"You don't have to say anything. Just that you're happy to be with me."

"I am. Of course I am." She lifted up and kissed him lightly on the lips.

He pulled her close. "That's all I ask," he whispered against her hair. He drew in a long breath, released her, and stepped back. A grin stretched across his mouth. "You know what other goodies I have in my bag?"

"Hmm?"

"Old movies. Some of the classics."

"Great. The stew needs to simmer for at least another hour. We could watch one until dinner is ready."

"See, that's what I love about you—you're so agreeable." He scooped up his bag and headed downstairs to the living area.

Tracy stood in the doorway of her bedroom, listening to Mark humming downstairs. He had no idea that the woman he was falling for didn't really exist, or rather existed only on paper. For the first time in longer than she could remember, she was actually beginning to feel joy, some happiness. But it couldn't be real, because Victoria Styles wasn't real.

She walked out of her bedroom and started for the stairs. For now she'd take all the happiness she could stand and deal with the rest later.

"What do you want to watch first?" she asked, coming up behind him. She slid her arms around his waist and pressed close.

He flipped through the stack of DVDs in his hand. In the months that she'd come to know Mark, she soon discovered he was a movie buff, especially a fan of old movies and thrillers. He could tell you exactly what star appeared in each film, the year it was made, and the name of the director without even blinking. Not to mention knowing every remake and how it stood up to the original. It was quite amazing, so she was always game to see what he had in store.

"You pick."

"How about some Hitchcock? I have *Vertigo* and *Strangers on a Train.*" He turned to her with wide-eyed enthusiasm. "Hitchcock was the master of suspense—you do know that, don't you?"

"Yes, dear. Doesn't everyone?" she teased.

"Not funny. So which one?"

"Hmm, *Strangers on a Train.* I don't think I've ever seen this one."

"You'll love it. It was originally based on the Patricia Highsmith novel. So many movies have emulated the theme behind this film. *A Kiss before Dying, Dial M for Murder,* another Hitchcock." He chuckled. "The old boy copied himself. Hmmm, let's see, *The Talented Mr. Ripley, Mortal Thoughts . . .*"

"What's the theme?"

He popped the DVD in the machine and pressed PLAY, then turned to her. "Exchange murders. Complete strangers kill off the other person's problem. Murders with no known link between the victim and the killer. Brilliant."

Of course, Mark being Mark had the original black-and-white version, and he was happy to explain Hitchcock's genius in using light to create effect and how that was one of the reasons why the old black-and-whites were some of the best movies made.

"They didn't rely on a lot of effects and explosions. Actors had to act, and you had to have a storyline strong enough to carry the movie. So much of what we see today is all created in a studio somewhere."

Tracy nestled closer to Mark. Much like her, she thought. Victoria Styles was created. She was the color version of her former self. Tracy Alexander was pure black-and-white with a little gray for effect.

The music cued and the movie began.

"SO WHAT DID YOU THINK?" Mark asked as they fixed their dinner plates in the kitchen.

"I thought it was great. I like all of Sir Hitchcock's films." She handed him a large soup bowl. The bottom she filled with rice, and Mark ladled the stew on top.

"Can't wait to sink my teeth into this."

"There's salad in the fridge. Would you take it out for me?"

"If you could ever live a different life, what would it be?" Mark asked out of the blue.

Tracy dropped the spoon on the floor. Momentarily flustered, she picked it up and washed it off in the sink. "Uh, what do you mean?"

"Well, you lived in New York, the big bad city, and worked at a small law office. If you had the chance, what other kind of life would you choose?"

"This one, I guess. Since this is where I am."

"Yeah, but you're here more for escape rather than real choice."

"I suppose." She was getting agitated. "What is it that you're really asking me?" She turned to face him, and he had the most unsettling look on his face, as if he were looking through her.

"If you somehow needed to redo your life, who would you be?" The corner of his mouth gently lifted.

For a moment, she couldn't think, didn't speak. She swallowed. "I really don't know. I suppose I'd have to think about it," she said in a weak response.

He shrugged. "Yeah—me, too, I guess. I always imagined that my life would be more exciting, maybe even a little dangerous."

She patted his shoulder and brushed by him. "You, my dear, watch too many movies!"

They laughed and returned to the living room to watch the next movie and savor their dinner.

By the time the sun had fully set, there was close to a foot of snow outside with no sign of the blizzard stopping. Mark and Tracy's bellies were full, and they'd opted to check out the news before watching another movie.

"Looks pretty treacherous out there," Mark said as the

weatherman on location was practically obliterated from view on the screen.

"Better him than me," Tracy muttered.

"You're bad." He pushed up from the couch. "Why don't you show me which windows need checking before it gets too late."

"Sure."

She followed him around the house, carrying the supplies while he weatherproofed the windows. It all felt so right to her. This is what couples did on a snowy afternoon—enjoyed each other. This was what Scott had wanted from her, but she'd been too consumed to see how much the little things mattered.

The odd sensation she'd experienced earlier in the kitchen was gone. She attributed her unease to the double life that she was leading, always being alert, suspicious of everyone.

The truth, she was afraid of what she was feeling. It felt right, and how could that be good?

"All done." He turned around. "You are a wonderful apprentice, young Jedi."

Tracy giggled. "You are too kind, Master Yoda."

"Become a Jedi one day you might," he teased, doing a pretty good impersonation of the green master of the *Star Wars* universe.

"Hey—" she wagged a finger "—if you ever want to give up your day job, you might have a shot at a second career."

He chuckled. "I'll keep that in mind."

Later, after making slow, passionate love, Tracy lay curled next to Mark and came to a decision. She was going to really give this relationship a chance. She was going to put her all into it and open her heart.

She closed her eyes, satisfied with her decision. As she began drifting off, the images of her wonderful day played like a film in her head.

Her eyes flew open. The missing piece of the puzzle suddenly fell into place: *exchange murders.* Her heart began racing. That's how they did it.

FOURTEEN

KIM STEPPED OUT of the pool and wrapped herself in a towel.

"We need to talk." Nicole was right behind her.

Kim glanced over her shoulder as she ran a towel through her hair. "What is it?"

"Let's go out back."

Kim huffed but went with Nicole anyway. They sat at one of the tables in the center of the yard beneath an umbrella.

Nicole immediately took out her pack of cigarettes and lit up.

Kim wrinkled her nose. "Well, you got me back here. What's going on?"

"I've been thinking about what that chick Charrie said about Tess."

Kim's blue eyes ran over Nicole's face. "And what about it?"

"If we'd stayed in the States, there was no way for Tess to ever be sure that we wouldn't, one, somehow get caught or, two, break down and tell someone."

"So what are you saying?"

"I'm saying that I think Tess got us down here to silence us for good."

Kim's expression pinched. "Why?" she asked in a monotone.

"We are the only two people other than her who know what went down, right?"

"Right."

"So what if Charrie is telling the truth? That Tess met with that guy and they are in it together? We know she had some kind of thing going on with him."

"It's not logical. Think about it. If Tess wanted us gone, she could have made that happen back in New York. Why bring us all the way out here to take care of something she could have done a long time ago, walked away from, and no one would be the wiser?"

Nicole breathed heavily. "Maybe. But somethin' still ain't sittin' right with me." She jerked her chin upward. "Don't make sense how she just up and left. And I don't like Ms. Charrie's attitude."

"How is she acting?"

"Like she knows somethin' I don't." She blew a cloud of smoke into the air.

Kim laughed. "Now you're being paranoid. She probably does know something you don't. And so what."

Nicole jumped up from her seat. "Fine. Blow it off." She crushed her cigarette beneath her sandaled foot. "But I'm tellin' you, shit stinks around here."

"Oh, there you two are." Charrie walked over, all smiles. "I wanted to talk with you both . . . about the business, how things are run, and what your responsibilities will be."

"Of course."

"Sure."

"Why don't we meet in the study in, say, twenty minutes." Before they had a chance to respond, she'd turned and walked away.

"*Puta,*" Nicole mumbled under her breath. With eyes cinched and her lips tightened to a thin line, she watched Charrie. "I don't care what you say, *chica*. I don't like that bitch."

"Let's hear what she has to say—then you and I can talk later, compare notes."

"Cool." She lit up another cigarette and then looked Kim up and down. "You need to hurry and put some clothes on, *mami*. You don't want to keep Ms. Thing waitin'."

THE LADIES GATHERED in the office twenty minutes later.

"I know you must be so confused about what's going on," Charrie began in a tone that was reserved for children.

"What I am is pissed," said Nicole. "I don't like being left in the dark. I came out here on the strength of Tess, and she's gone. You claim she had to go away on business and that leaves you in charge. You said that she's planning something with that guy, something that has to do with us."

"That's right. And I am dealing with things the way Tess would have. She needs to think that things are going along as normal. That neither of you nor I suspect anything out of the ordinary."

Nicole lifted her chin and folded her arms in front of her. "So what's the deal?"

"The both of you will be assisting me in the day-to-day operations, just the way Tess planned."

"So we just wait like sitting ducks until something happens?" Nicole challenged.

Charrie almost laughed out loud. She knew that one would jump at the bait. "Do you have a better idea?"

"I'm a businesswoman, Charrie," said Kim. "I've run a major corporation for more than a decade. One thing that I do know is that when you're running a business and you're not aware of the small details, you will get screwed." She drew in a breath. "How do I know? From experience, not from a textbook. I turned over the reins to someone who I thought I could trust, and also to appease them, make them feel valuable. But when the cards were put on the table, my company had been taken away from me, brick by brick. I'll never make that mistake again. I don't intend to get involved in anything anymore and not know *all* the little details and *all* the little details of everyone involved. Tess may be a lot of things, but one thing is certain: She is a businesswoman, pure and simple. A shrewd one."

Nicole wanted to applaud when she saw the tight bitch-slapped look on Charrie's face.

"I'm sure you've had your share of bad experiences. So have we." She lowered her head for a moment then looked at them, her expression apologetic. "The truth of the matter is . . . I don't know what Tess has planned. But I do know that she never leaves loose ends. And for whatever reason, you two are loose ends. If she even gets a whiff that you know, that something is out of sync . . . there's no telling what she might do." She waited. "The decision is up to you. You came here to start over, to make money. If you could have done that back in New York, you would have stayed. But you're here at her bidding."

She focused on Kim. "You said you lost everything once before. If Tess has her way, you'll lose it all again or worse." She turned to Nicole. "Tess is the only one who stands in the way of you getting what you want."

"What are you saying?" Kim asked.

"Take it any way you wish. No one knows Tess the way I do. And I'm telling you from experience, Tess will never let you have what she does. Never. Why do you really think she up and left?" She glanced from one to the other. "So that whatever she has up her sleeve, she won't be in the vicinity when it happens."

Nicole flinched.

Charrie pressed home her point. "She wants you to think that everything is fine and rock you right to sleep."

"You've been with her all this time, shared in all the riches," Nicole said. "Why are you so gung ho about us turning on her? From everything I can see, you've done damned well for yourself because of her. So why now?"

Charrie's eyes suddenly filled. "I've never had an ally before." Her voice cracked. "Never had anyone that I could turn to. I've been trapped in this life, tied to Tess. I have no family, no friends. I've walked in her shadows for years, doing her bidding. I've seen what she is capable of. And for the first time I have a chance. You have a chance." She sniffed. "I'm sorry." She turned her head away and waited.

Kim stood up. "We'll get back to you."

Nicole snatched a glance at Kim and then got up as well.

Charrie nodded her head. "She's ruthless and she's brilliant."

Nicole and Kim walked to the door.

"Wait." Charrie wrote something down on a piece of paper. She handed it to Kim. "It's Tess's number."

Kim took the paper, gave Charrie a long hard look, then walked out.

"What do you think?" Nicole asked as they headed down the hallway.

Kim looked straight ahead. *If Tess can kill her own sister, she is capable of anything.* "I think that if we want to stay alive, we need to get rid of Tess before she gets rid of us."

FIFTEEN

VINCENT PULLED INTO the parking lot of the motel and cut off the engine. He sat in the car for a few moments, thinking about his meeting with Charrie. Something didn't sit right with him, but he couldn't put his finger on it just yet.

He got out of the car and was walking toward the back entrance when he saw a figure emerge from two cars away. His first instinct was to go for his gun, but he didn't have one.

"I understand you've been looking for me," came the voice. "I hoped you'd believed I'd gone."

"Good of you to come," he said with caution, immediately recognizing the voice that had haunted his dreams.

"I didn't shoot you. I needed you to know that."

Vincent stood still as Tess approached. His entire body tensed. She was right in front of him.

"I didn't do it. You have to believe me."

"Why should I believe you?"

"Because I'm telling the truth," she said simply. "And I want to know who did it as badly as I know you do."

"How did you know where to find me?"

"I took a chance. It was the closest place to where we . . . had to meet that night." Her eyes ran over his face down to his torso. "How are you? Why did you leave the doctor's place?"

"You don't have a gun, do you?"

She gave him a wicked smile. "Always."

He shook his head and took her arm. "Come inside. We have a lot to talk about."

She followed him to his room.

"Nice place," she said, half-joking. "Nothing like your boat back home."

He turned, and the memories they shared played in their eyes. He glanced away. "Make yourself comfortable and, uh, take your gun out of your bag and put it where I can see it."

"You don't trust me."

"I don't trust guns."

"Fine." She went into her handbag and took out her pistol then placed it on the nightstand.

Vincent came over, picked it up, and put it on top of the television on the other side of the room.

"Feel better now?"

"Much." He eased down into the chair by the window, grimacing slightly as he did so.

"Are you still in pain?"

"A little. But it's bearable. Nothing that a couple of aspirin won't cure."

"Why did you come after me, Vincent? Why couldn't you have just left it alone?"

"I had to. After you left without a word, I couldn't get you out of my head, off my mind. I flipped between rage to pity, loss to betrayal, and back again. Every day. Nothing and no one has ever affected me like that." He looked at her a long time. "Why did you leave, Tess? Why did you leave *me*?"

Her throat was so tight, she could barely speak. "I had to. You left me no choice. I found out who you were. I couldn't let you turn me in."

Vincent blinked. "I guess we both were deceiving each other. You weren't who you claimed to be either."

"And you knew that from the beginning."

"I wasn't sure. I wasn't. All I knew was that you were this hot, fabulous, funny, sexy woman that I wanted to know. I wasn't sure until we made love for the first time and I saw the tattoo on your hip."

She snickered. "I always thought men didn't kiss and tell. Someone apparently did. You'd have to get real up close and personal to know that tiny detail."

He flicked his brow. "Yes, I was sent to hunt you down by the DA's office and bring you in. I'd been working vice for years. Avery Powell and I go way back. He thought I'd be the perfect draw."

"Apparently you were." She got up and began to pace. "So was all the wining and dining and sweet words part of the job, too?" She spun toward him, her arms tightly folded.

"At first, yes. But not after I'd gotten to know you. It was all real."

She lowered her head.

"If I wanted to take you in, I could have."

"And if I wanted to kill you, I could have," she tossed back. "I could have left you there to bleed to death."

"Why didn't you?"

She turned away. "I couldn't."

"Why? Tell me why."

The words were in her head, in the center of her chest, in her throat, and then moving across her lips. "Because I realized that I love you."

He got up and came to stand in front of her. He made her look up at him. "The same reason I couldn't turn you in."

Her heart slammed so hard in her chest, she couldn't breathe for a moment. "What . . . are you saying?"

"I'm saying that I love you, Tess. I love you, even knowing all that I know about you. I love the idea of wanting to know more about you. I didn't come here to bring you back. I came here to convince you never to leave me again."

"Why should I believe you?" she asked softly, the hint of a smile forming around her wide mouth.

"Because I'm telling you the truth," he said, echoing her.

She drew in a long, slow breath. "So where do we go from here?"

"The man in me says, get the hell out of here and start a life with you somewhere far, far away. But the detective in me says to find out who tried to kill me—or you—or we'll never be able to rest well or step out in the street without looking over our shoulder."

Tess sucked in her bottom lip. "I know you're right. I've been racking my brain, trying to think who would have done it. More important, how did anyone know both of us were going to be there?"

"Exactly. The only person who knows I'm here is Avery. It wouldn't suit his purposes to have me shot."

"That leaves me." She looked into his eyes.

"I was hoping not to arrive at that conclusion, but it's the only one that makes any sense—or at least as much as it can. They were either after you directly and missed or they wanted it to appear that you did it. Maybe they hoped that someone would come running and find you there. Whatever the reasoning, you were set up."

Tess moved across the room and sat down.

"Let's go back over that night. Tell me what happened from the time I called you."

Tess looked upward, searching her memory. "Charrie took the call. After you and I hung up, I told . . . them I had to leave. I got my gun, got in my car, and drove out here. I just got a glimpse of you standing in the moonlight when the shot fired. I ran over to you, and when I saw that you were still alive, I had to figure out what to do. The only person that I could trust was Winston Sinclair."

Vincent's eyes widened like saucers. "The fuckin' prime minister?" he asked in disbelief.

"Yes. Winston and I go way back."

"Lady, you sure travel in high circles. So who was the guy who was taking care of me?"

"A friend of Winston's, a doctor."

"Okay so we've backtracked your actions. If we decide that it wasn't me they were after and it was you, the question is why? Who has a grudge?"

"No one that I know of."

"Who has something to gain by getting you out of the way?"

Nicole? Kim? I won't even mention their names. Never. How could they benefit by getting rid of her? Charrie would never let that happen. *Charrie.*

"What? What is it? I see it in your eyes."

"The only one I can think of is Charrie. She knows everything there is to know about the business. Everything. She knows where the accounts are, how we hire our 'staff,' how we screen our clientele. She knows all of my connections, who to call and when." She started feeling ill. She shook off the ugly sensation. "I took her in. Taught her everything." She stared directly at him. "She never worked . . . not like that. I wouldn't let her. I treated her . . . like my daughter, my younger sister. She wouldn't do that."

Vincent drew in a breath. "Tess, someone in your organization has been feeding information to the DA's office for months. Whoever the informant is, she worked with your sister and then—"

"You knew Tracy was my sister?"

"No. Not at first. Avery finally put it together."

"So whoever this person is started giving information to Avery."

He nodded. "Yes."

"But if the business falls, if it's someone inside, they lose everything, too."

"Monetary stuff, but they'd never spend a day in jail. They'd get immunity for turning state's evidence."

She covered her face with her hands. "Could someone resent me that much?"

"Apparently someone does. And the only common denominator is Charrie."

"No. I won't believe that."

"Tess . . ." He reached across the space and took her hands. "Look at me." She did. "Forget all this. Leave with me. If it is Charrie, then so be it. We can make a new life someplace else. Someplace where neither she nor Avery will ever find us. I can make that happen. The reality is, what can you do?"

Her mind raced. Charrie. If it was Charrie and she had gone so far as to try to kill her or set her up for murder, there was no telling what she would do to Nikki and Kim if her goal was to run the business totally on her own.

She brought Nicole and Kimberly into this. She'd sealed their fate from the moment she set eyes on them in the doctor's office. She'd convinced them that getting rid of their problems was the only solution. She'd convinced them because that's what she did; it was what she was good at, convincing people of what they want, their most secret desires.

Had it not been for her, they would have gone on with their lives and lived them the best way they could. But she had intervened, and whatever the fates had planned for them was changed forever.

She couldn't just walk away. She couldn't leave them unknowing. She might be a high-priced whore, but she was also a loyal friend.

"I can't leave with you."

"What? Why not?"

"I . . . can't. Not now. Maybe never."

"You're not making sense. I'm offering an out. A life."

"There are people here that I owe. I can't abandon them."

Vincent visibly withdrew. His eyes darkened and his hard body grew taut. "I don't want to lose you again. What about me? I've risked my career, my own freedom for you. Because I didn't bring you in, I can never go back. I can never resume my life. I'm willing to do that for you. What are you willing to do for me?"

"Vincent, please—"

"No, Tess. *Please.*" He grabbed her by the shoulders. "Come with me. We can start over on one of the other islands. Avery knows we're here. He may send someone else to find you, force you to go back."

"The U.S. has no jurisdiction here."

"No. But Aruba has extradition laws. You can be forced to leave and be taken back."

She pulled away.

He grabbed her again. "But there are places that can't happen. And even so, Avery isn't so blinded by ambition and ego that he would waste taxpayers' dollars chasing you around the globe. His ego would be hurt, but he'd survive."

She listened, but she wouldn't relent. "I understand. I do. But if you do love me and you want a life with me, let me do what I need to do."

"What is it between you and them . . . whoever *they* are?"

"I . . . can't tell you. All I can say is that I owe a debt. And I pay my debts."

Vincent's hard stance slowly eased. His tight shoulders dropped He looked upward and then down at her. "All right. We'll do it your way. For now."

She reached up and kissed him tenderly on the mouth. "Thank you." She waited a beat. "Tomorrow isn't promised, but we have tonight."

Vincent pulled her close. Her body was flush with his, and a scorching heat raced through him. He felt her tremble ever so slightly—and just knowing that he could evoke that kind of reaction from a woman like Tess intensified his need for her.

He didn't realize how desperately he'd wanted and missed her until that very instant. It was overwhelming. When he leaned down and kissed her the way he remembered kissing her, nothing else mattered. Nothing else but having her again—entering her body and making it his again.

When he touched her bare skin and heard her sigh, he knew

that everything he'd sacrificed would be worth it just to have her again, to hold and love her again.

Tess made him feel both weak and powerful every time she moved her hips, tightened and opened her thighs, offered up the tips of her breasts, whispered his name, stroked his back, and told him that she loved him. He couldn't let her go—not ever again.

SHE LOVED HIM. She did. The validation was both frightening and comforting in its strength. Love was not something that Tess Mc-Donald allowed in her life. There was no place for it. Love had been her great betrayer. Whenever she opened her heart and truly gave of herself, she paid dearly for it. First Winston, now Charrie. Would her love for Vincent betray her as well?

At that moment, as she felt him surge against her, she didn't care about anything but giving all of herself to him. In Vincent's embrace, her past no longer existed, her present was idyllic, and her future welcomed possibility.

Vincent braced his weight on his forearms and looked into her eyes. "That was incredible."

"It was," she whispered, and felt his cock jerk inside her.

"Hmmm," he murmured against her neck, and kissed the soft spot right behind her ear. "It's different between us, Tess."

She stroked his head. "What do you mean?"

"This isn't some flash in the pan, some passing thing. We're risking everything to be together. That means something. I know it does for me."

"I've never had anyone willing to do what you're doing for me. Never." *Not even Winston,* she thought. "Maybe that's why I chose the life that I did, looking for something, someone to care about me, even if it was all an illusion."

"None of that matters to me. The past is gone. There's nothing to be done about that. What's important is the *now*."

She pulled him closer and held on. At that moment she felt so close to him, almost a part of his body. She wanted to purge herself of everything, to tell him about Troy and Trust, about what she'd done. But she knew she could never burden him with that knowledge. The secret was hers to bear.

"There's something that you should know," Vincent said.

"What?"

"Your sister is alive."

SIXTEEN

TESS PUSHED HIM off her. She sat straight up in bed. "What? I was at her funeral. I saw her in the casket!" Her temples pounded. This was some trick, some gimmick to make her confess. She moved away from him, accusation and suspicion burning in her eyes.

Vincent reached for her hand and she snatched it away. "It's true. Listen to me," he said.

"You knew?" she said, incredulity making her voice warble.

"Yes."

"And you sat there and listened to me talk and you never said a word. How could you? Did you suddenly have an attack of conscience after a good fuck?" She jumped out of bed, dragging the sheet with her. She wrapped it around her body, shielding herself.

All this time the guilt over her sister's death had borne down on her. All for nothing.

"So the whole shooting was a hoax? Why?"

"No. The shooting was real. Your sister nearly died. That's all true. But when she pulled through and Avery realized that it had been a hit, he shipped Tracy out and put her under protective custody."

Tess wandered around the room in a daze. *Tracy is alive.* "How long have you known?"

"I've always known. But I couldn't say anything—not even to you." He drew in a breath. "I was supposed to come here and tell you that we found your sister's killer and that we wanted you back in the States for the trial. We do have the guy, but Tracy is far from dead."

"That's how you were going to get me to come back?"

"Yes. There are only four people who know that: Avery, me, the agent that placed her, and now you."

"Where is she?"

He shook his head. "That I can't tell you. For her protection."

"New life? New home?"

"Yes, and a new name."

Tess nodded, and slowly her pain began to ease. She never got a chance to thank Tracy for warning her, for saving her, and she'd always regretted it. Maybe now—someday, somehow—she would be able to show her gratitude.

"She's safe and she's happy—at least as happy as Tracy can be when she's not fighting crime."

"If you can do it without compromising her, tell her thank you for me."

She'd figured out long ago that it was neither Kim nor Nicole who'd shot her sister. It wasn't their style. But Tracy's death was the catalyst that had set their plan of murder into motion. That plan had rippled and grown, taking on a life of its own. Where would it all end?

The next morning Tess prepared to leave.

"What are you planning to do—can you at least tell me that?" Vincent asked her while she dressed.

"I need to warn some friends, and after I do that and I know that they will be all right, I'll be back." She walked over to the television, took down her gun, stuck it in her handbag, and pulled out another one. "I think you lost this," she said handing the other weapon over to him.

"You're a piece of work."

"So I hear."

"How will I know—?"

"I'll call you as soon as I can. I promise." She reached up and kissed him then quickly walked out, closing the door gently behind her.

Out in the parking lot, she sat in her car, weeping. The ache in her heart was so painful, she thought it would break. Not until now, alone, had she allowed herself to consider that it could only have been Charrie behind everything. Tess was rocked to her core. She'd put up a good front for Vincent, letting him think the betrayal had rolled off her shoulders. But it hadn't—it was like a hot knife jammed into her gut, digging deeper with every breath she took.

She must be getting too old for the game, letting emotions get the best of her. That wasn't Tess McDonald. At least it never had been. Had she discovered this about Charrie five years ago, she would have cut her off without blinking. But now, she was no longer simply moving through life. Tess was a part of it, living it and breathing it, and that meant having feelings. It was terrifying.

Her cell phone rang. Tess frowned. There were only two people who had her number: Charrie and now Vincent.

She answered. "Yes?"

"This is Kim. We need to talk."

"Kim, I was going to call you."

"Sure. That's why you disappeared without a word. Brought us all the way out here . . . for what, exactly, Tess? To make sure that we were never seen or heard from again? Was that the plan, you and Vincent?"

She flinched. How did Kim know about Vincent by name? "You have it all wrong."

"Meet us in a hour." She told Tess where to go, and hung up.

If Tess had had any doubts that Charrie was pulling the strings, they were gone now. The only person who knew she had gone to see Vincent was Charrie, and she'd gone and told Kim and Nicole. The question was, why?

It was obviously a setup. They wanted to meet on the outskirts of town, up in the hills. Tess thought about going back and telling Vincent, but decided against confiding in him. He would try to stop her. No matter how things went down, she had to face them and at least have the chance to explain.

"EVERYONE ALREADY THINKS she's gone," Kim was saying as they drove up the winding road to the meeting place. "If she doesn't come back, no one will ever think we had anything to do with it." She turned to Nikki. "Just like Tess taught us. I checked out the spot. There's nothing around for miles. And it's straight down the rocky cliff into the ocean."

Nikki took it all in. She'd lived a tough life, the fast life of the street. She'd seen death and destruction on a regular basis. She considered herself tough, able to handle anything. But actually putting her hands on someone to kill them—that was something else altogether. Sure, she'd been responsible for Troy Benning's death. She'd rigged his car, knowing that after fifteen minutes he'd have no brakes. But she didn't have to see it happen. She never had to look in his face, see the fear or accusation. She never had to put her hands on him. Kim had done that, though. She'd walked up to Trust and pushed him over a balcony like a sack of dirty laundry. Who was really the ruthless one, Tess or Kim?

"What did you tell Charrie?" Nikki asked.

"I told her that we would take care of our problem."

Nikki stared out the window. Who would ever have imagined that it would come to this? A little more than a year ago, they were all complete strangers. Their sense of betrayal and feelings of desperation drove them to do the unthinkable. Tess had been the mastermind, true. She'd convinced them that it was possible. And now the students hunted the teacher. What next? When they got rid of this loose end, would they then turn on each other?

"That's the spot up ahead," Kim said, drawing Nikki back from her dark thoughts.

"I don't see her."

"She'll come." Kim parked the car, and they waited.

seventeen

TRACY'S THOUGHTS RACED. All night she'd tossed ideas around, rearranging all the pieces of information. Had Mark not been there, she would have gotten up and gone through her files. She knew that the answers were in there, and only pure chance—the movie—had alerted her. *Exchange murders.* What she needed was to find the one element that tied them all together.

"Are you okay?" Mark asked. "You've been quiet and distracted all morning."

"I'm fine." She smiled. "Guess I'm already getting stir-crazy." She went to the window.

The blizzard had wound down to flurries, and the forecasters predicted it would clear up entirely over the next few hours. But there was at least two feet of snow covering everything as far as the eye could see.

Mark walked up behind her and put his arms around her waist. "We won't have a chance like this anytime soon." He kissed the back of her neck.

"A time like what?" she asked absently.

He took her shoulders and turned her around to face him. "What is it?"

"Nothing, really." She touched his cheek. "I'm sorry. You're right. We should make the most of this time together."

"Wanna help me dig out my car?"

"Sure."

They spent over an hour digging out his truck and clearing a path in the driveway. By the time they came back inside, they were freezing, giddy with laughter, and wet.

"Whew. Not as young as I used to be," Mark said, stomping his feet at the door. He hung up his coat.

"None of us are," she said, laughing. "I'm going to warm up that stew."

"Perfect. I want to get out of these clothes and take a quick hot shower."

"Go on ahead."

"Yes, ma'am." He trotted upstairs.

Tracy set the pot of stew on the stove, and when she heard the shower come on upstairs, she quickly lowered the flame and went to her home office.

She found her files and she started with Nicole Perez. After scanning the information, Tracy took down the name of her parole officer. Next, she searched Kimberly Shepherd-Benning's file. Her instincts told her that finances were somehow involved. She got the name of Kim's accountant. Tess must be the link connecting them all, but how and why?

"Shower's all yours!" she heard Mark call out as he came downstairs.

"Thanks." She shoved the folder back in the file drawer and put away the phone numbers. Excitement rushed through her. She hadn't felt energized like this since she'd left New York. She was on the brink of putting it all together. She could feel it.

She headed to the living room but stopped short. This same exhilaration, this grinding desire to win at all costs . . . She'd already been down this road. Her relentless quest to discover the identity of Madame X had consumed her once to the exclusion of everything else. She'd found what she was looking for, and it nearly destroyed her. She found her sister. And here again, Tess was at the heart of two suspicious deaths. She knew that as surely as she knew her own name. Would finding the truth be worth it this time?

"Hey." Mark was looking at her quizzically. "Why are you standing there like that?" He ran a towel over his damp hair.

She focused on Mark. "Oh, nothing. Thought I heard the snowplows outside. Come on, the stew should be warm."

"Always better on day two," Mark said later as he wolfed down his food. "Since it looks like we're stuck together for another afternoon, what do you want to do?"

He waited but got no response. He put his spoon down. "Vicky, what's wrong? You've been acting weird all morning."

"Uh? Oh." She forced a smile. "I'm sorry, just distracted, that's all."

"Want to talk about it? Maybe I can help."

"Just thinking about my life back in New York."

"Do you miss it?"

"Sometimes."

"But I thought you said you were all right with being here."

"I am." She shrugged. "I guess sometimes I get a little home-sick."

"That's to be expected." He paused. "Why don't we plan to take a trip to New York, in the spring when the weather breaks?"

She knew from her time with Mark that he was not a big-city kind of guy. He'd spent his entire life in their small town. His family was here, he'd gone to school here, and he worked here.

"Mark . . . what if you were involved with someone and you found out that they were not who you thought they were?"

"What do you mean?"

"Someone really close to you. Someone you really cared about."

"That all depends on who I found out they were, I suppose, and what their relationship was to me." He gave her a curious look. "If I cared enough about them, I'd take all of that into consideration."

She was thoughtful for a moment, debating on how much to share.

"I wasn't always the straight-up-and-down good Samaritan firefighter."

She stared at him. "You weren't?"

"No. And I didn't actually grow up here like I said I did."

She frowned. "You didn't?"

"I grew up in Atlanta." He blew out a breath. "I probably should have told you this a long time ago, but I didn't know how you would take it. And then you've always been kind of tight-lipped about your life prior to coming here. I thought maybe I should leave well enough alone."

"So, you grew up in Atlanta instead of Colorado. That's no big deal. I still don't understand why you would keep that a secret."

"I was married."

Her eyes widened. "Married?"

He nodded. "To Theresa Morgan. We went to high school together, got married right after graduation, against both of our parents' wishes. My folks wanted me to go to college and make something of myself." He chuckled without humor. "But I was in love . . . and Theresa was pregnant."

Her mouth opened to respond, but she couldn't find the words. *He has a child? Where is it, and where is his wife?*

"I was pretty wild back then, and determined to live my life the way I wanted. So we got married. She had the baby about seven months later. To say it was a struggle is putting it mildly. I didn't have any skills, and Theresa had to stay home with the baby because we couldn't afford a sitter. Our parents wanted nothing to do with us. Her dad was a preacher, and as far as he was concerned, Theresa was going straight to hell." His face contorted for a moment.

"Anyway, I took whatever odd jobs I could. I finally wound up working for a gas station and Stop-N-Shop, pumping gas and fixing flat tires. One day some old-school friends rolled up. We got to talking, and they convinced me to help them rob the place."

"Oh . . . Mark."

"Things were so bad at home. We had no money. Barely any food. Me and Theresa fought just about every day. I figured it wasn't much but it would pay for something. So . . . we planned to do it on a Saturday night. I got off work as usual, signed out, and hooked up with the guys. Around midnight we came back and stuck the place up. Got away with about three hundred dollars to split between four people." He shook his head. "We probably got about a mile away before the police caught up with us. I spent three years in jail for armed robbery. Theresa came to see me every chance she got." He swallowed, and his eyes grew misty. "One day when she was driving back home, she got hit by a tractor trailer and was killed . . . along with my daughter."

"Oh my God. Mark . . ."

"When I finally got out, I was like a zombie. I didn't care about anything. I blamed myself for what happened. Then I got wild and crazy, drinking, drugging, running from woman to woman. One day when I was sure I was going out of my mind, I ran into Theresa's mother on the street. I hadn't seen her almost eight years. She took one look at me and brought me home with her. She got me into rehab, took me to church every Sunday, but most important, she forgave me. She said it took her a long time to get over the loss of Theresa—first to me and then to the tragedy. But that she finally realized that harboring ill will is like a cancer. It can eat you alive, she said, and that maybe if she had been more forgiving, more understanding, she could have been there for us and I would never have felt the need to do what I did and Theresa and her grandchild would still be alive.

"When she said that, it was like the weight of the world had been lifted from my shoulders. I felt like I could breathe again. She said it took her a long time to accept that circumstances often drive people to do things they never would have done otherwise. Forgiveness and acceptance of another person are the greatest gifts you can give them or yourself."

He looked across the table at Tracy. "We can't see what drives another person or what kinds of hurts and fears live in their hearts. Forgiving myself for my past opened up my future. I wanted to live again. So, I moved here, went back to school, took the test for the fire department, and started a new life. . . . I've never told anyone what I've just told you."

"I'm touched that you trust me enough to share that painful part of your life."

"Yes, I *do* trust you." He looked directly at her. "And you can trust me, too. I trust you because I want you to be a part of my life, Vicky, a *real* part of my life. I want you to know me, battle scars and all. I want to take a chance on loving again, being in love, and getting it back."

Tracy looked up. "Thank you. More than you know."

Mark smiled softly. "Did that answer your question?"

"Yes, it did."

"Well, whenever you're ready to talk—really talk—I'm ready to listen." He lowered his head and continued eating. "It's all about trust."

Trust was hard for Tracy to handle. She'd spent the better part of her life dealing with folks whose M. O. didn't involve trust. She'd dealt with liars, murderers, drug dealers, rapists. Some of the most mild-mannered-looking folks were serial killers. A man who wouldn't hurt a dog could beat his wife to death. She took no one at face value, no matter what they said or how sincere they appeared. Why should she?

She watched Mark as he ate. He was handsome, warm, funny, intelligent, a hard worker. And according to him, he was a man who had lost not only his family but also a large part of himself.

Mark was a man redeemed, someone to take home to the family—or so he seemed. Old instincts died hard, and as much as she wanted to, she wasn't quite ready to let him in. Avery's words of warning rang in her head: *You can't trust anyone.*

eighteen

Tess had no idea what Nikki and Kim had planned, but she knew it wasn't going to go down easy. She made the turn and began her ascent along the winding path. The closer she drew to her destination, the more apprehensive she became. The area was isolated, with a magnificent view of the ocean. She slowed, pulled off the road and came to a stop. She reached in her purse, looked at her phone. Call Vincent, her mind screamed. Tell him where you are.

The silver handle of her pistol gleamed in the blazing sunlight. She took it out, checked the chamber. It was fully loaded. She took off the safety and put it back in her bag, keeping the zipper open for easy access. She continued up the incline until she spotted a car. Her heart pumped a little faster.

She had to convince them of the truth, or she knew that without a doubt, they would kill her.

Kim and Nikki turned at the sound of a car's engine.

"That must be her," Kim said. She turned to Nikki. "Don't forget the plan. It's either her or us."

Nikki tossed her long ponytail over her shoulder and nodded. This was like the days back in the streets of East Harlem. The setting may be all picturesque and shit, but the game was the same. The showdown. The spoils would go to the last man standing. She stole a glance over the cliff and watched the ocean slam up against the rocks below. Hell of a fall. By the time anyone found Tess, if anyone ever did, she'd be unrecognizable.

Tess cut off the engine, stepped out of the car, and looped the strap of her bag over her shoulder. She wished she'd worn something better than sandals. The last thing she needed was to lose her footing. She started up the rest of hill.

"Good to see you, Tess," Kim said, her face as still as the rocks below.

"Kim. Nikki." She stopped a few feet in front of them.

"Why don't you toss your bag over there." Nikki jutted her chin toward the right. She'd been in enough showdowns to know that the opponent never came empty-handed. She was pretty sure Tess had more in her bag then lip gloss.

Tess looked from one to the other then finally tossed the bag aside. "Happy?"

"Very," Kim said. She stared at Tess, this woman whom she'd reluctantly come to admire for her business savvy, raw nerve, and intellect. And now she was forced to get rid of her to save herself. Her conscience twitched for a moment. Sure, she'd also conspired to get rid of Troy to save herself, her company, and Stephanie. In the end, she still wound up with nothing. Not this time.

"Why'd you do it, Tess? Why did you bring us here?"

"You know why I brought you here. I owed you. I owed both of you."

"And you pay us back by betraying us? What's the real reason you got us here, so that you could conveniently make us disappear along with any trace of what happened back in New York?" Kim pressed.

"No. You got it wrong this time, Ms. Executive. You pride yourself in always picking the right people for the job, trusting your instincts. Do your instincts really tell you that I would do something like that? If I wanted to be sure you never talked, I could have done that in New York, where all my connections were solid. I could have made you disappear as if you never existed. And as much as you want to believe anything else, you know what I'm saying is the truth."

"The truth!" Kim sputtered a nasty laugh. "The truth is that you are exactly what you said you were, a person who could make people believe . . . believe in the dream . . . believe in the fantasy. It's what you do. Remember? In other words, a liar."

"You're right. It is what I do." She moved to the left. "I make people's dreams come true, if only for an hour. But I'm not lying to you now."

"Why should we believe you?" Kim shouted. "Charrie told us everything. She told us that you went to meet Vincent. The very man you claimed to have left behind shows up here, and you disappear. Charrie told us she overheard your conversation. She said you told him we knew everything. You said you were going to end it all, when you left the party. But he shows up at the villa days later. And you pretend to have gone away on business. What were you planning, Tess, huh? What?"

"Don't you see? Charrie is behind everything. The night I left, I did go to meet Vincent. I was going to end things. But before I could, someone shot him."

"You're lying." Kim moved closer. "He showed up at the villa. Charrie said so."

"I took him to a friend of mine. He got Vincent a doctor. I stayed with him, that's why I didn't come back. When I thought he was stable, I left."

"Why didn't you come back to the villa?" Nikki asked.

"At the time, I wasn't sure if whoever shot Vincent was after me or him. And since I never had the chance to talk to Vincent, I knew that once he was well enough, he would come looking for me at the villa, which could lead him to both of you. I had to pretend that I'd gone away."

"You're all smoke and mirrors, Tess. Nothing more. That's a great story," Kim said. She flashed Nikki a look, and they both lunged at Tess, throwing her to the ground.

"Anyone who could kill her own sister is capable of anything," Kim ground out, grabbing Tess by the ankles.

Tess kicked, catching Kim in the side. Kim howled, regained her hold, and dragged Tess toward the edge. Nikki grabbed Tess's arms as Tess struggled violently.

"I didn't kill my sister!" She twisted and jerked her body, struggling to free herself. She saw her purse but knew she couldn't get to it.

"You're a liar! Her name was in the envelope. You picked your own sister's name," Kim spat, and heaved herself up, pulling Tess by the legs.

Tess saw the edge of the cliff, and everything she'd ever done seemed to play before her eyes.

"My sister isn't dead!"

"Liar!"

Tess fought with all her strength. She twisted her head and sank her teeth into Nikki's hand. Nikki screamed, lost her grip, and the momentum made Kim stumble backwards. The terrified look on her face as she tried to balance herself on the edge of the cliff froze them all in place for a split second.

"No!" Tess shouted, and scrambled to her feet. She reached Kim just as she went over the edge. "Help me!" Tess screamed out to Nikki, who seemed unable to move. "Help me. I can't pull her up."

Kim's fingers dug into the dirt; her feet scrambled to gain some purchase. Pieces of rock fell to the waters below. Tess had Kim's arm in one hand and the front of her shirt in the other. The seam ripped. As she slipped, Kim screamed.

The shriek jolted Nikki from her stupor. She ran to the edge.

"Don't let me fall, please," Kim begged.

When Nikki finally grabbed Kim's other arm, she and Tess dragged Kim to safety. Kim shuddered and heaved with sobs.

Nikki sat with her knees drawn up to her chest, rocking back and forth. "Her funeral was on television. I saw it myself," she said in a distant voice. "I saw it."

"She's not dead," Tess repeated.

Kim slowly drew herself up. She looked at Nikki and then at Tess. "You saved my life," she whispered.

Tess opened her eyes and turned her head toward Kim.

"You could have let me fall."

"I didn't let you fall down that elevator shaft back in New York. You think I would get you all the way out here to let you fall off a fuckin' cliff."

"I didn't want to believe you'd hurt us," Nikki muttered. She looked at Tess with tears in her eyes. "But Charrie . . ."

Tess gingerly sat up. "Charrie learned everything she knows from me. Including the art of persuasion." She turned to Kim. "Smoke and mirrors."

"Why?" Kim said, frowning in confusion. "Why would she want to set you up?"

Tess breathed out slowly. "That's what I came here to tell you."

As the trio sat on top of the hill, Tess explained as well as she could what Charrie had engineered long before coming to Aruba.

"When I got the first call that my place was going to be raided, all I thought about was being thankful that I had friends. It was right after we closed up shop that the district attorney started getting more information on me. That's how Vincent found me in Brooklyn."

"Vincent works for the DA's office?" Nikki asked.

Tess nodded. "At least he did."

"Shit," she sputtered.

"So of course she led them here," Kim added.

"Apparently."

"But why? I mean, it doesn't make sense. Why would she turn on you like that?"

"That's what I've been trying to figure out. The only thing I can come up with is that she finally got tired of living in my shadow. She wanted it all. And if she couldn't get rid of me legally, she'd find another way. Through the two of you."

"Wait," Kim said. "If that's anywhere near true, then why would she shoot Vincent instead of you?"

"I don't know. Maybe she aimed and missed. Maybe she wanted me to take the fall for it." She shook her head. "I just don't know."

They were all silent.

"Does Vincent know about . . . Troy and Trust?" Nikki asked with trepidation in her voice.

"No. And I'll never tell him. No one knows."

"Not even Charrie?"

"Not even Charrie."

"How can you be sure?"

"I am," she said with confidence. "And no one must ever find out."

"But if you didn't kill your sister, then who did?"

"From what Vincent told me, it was a hit. Plain and simple. And because of the plan we had between us when Tracy was gunned down, we each thought it was one of us who did it and—"

"And carried out the rest," Kim said, finishing the sentence.

"So that means, in this whole ugly mess, you're the only one with clean hands," Nikki said. "You got the empty envelope that night." She gave Tess a hard look.

Tess pressed her lips together and nodded. "Yes, I did."

They'd burned the fourth envelope. The one with Tracy's name in it. Lucky? She didn't feel lucky. Not at all.

"And all along, at the very least I thought we were all on the same playing field," Kim said. "Humph, you really screwed us, didn't you?"

"I had no way of knowing how it was going to play out. None of us did. It was a chance we all agreed to take. And it's a guilt that I've lived with ever since. I didn't know how you managed to do what you did to Trust and Troy, and I didn't want to know. But when Vincent called the villa, I believed it was finally my chance to balance the scales, so that there would never be a question of loyalty."

Nikki glared at Tess, and her beautiful face contorted. "But you didn't shoot him. You didn't kill him. You even got him a doctor. *Why?*"

"I . . . I love him. I was going to leave with him. Go away for good. Leave everything to you both and Charrie." She spoke with effort. "Vincent is the first man who knew who I was, what I was about, and loved me anyway. He didn't come here to take me in, he came here to tell me that. He risked his career, his very life for me. I've never had that before."

Kim let out a slow breath of sorrow and defeat. "Well, where do we go from here? What next? I've come so far from the person I once was, I don't even recognize myself anymore."

"Does Charrie know about this?"

"She knew we intended to meet you," Nikki said.

"But she didn't ask for details."

Tess nodded. "The only way to try to salvage anything is to finally smoke her out. Otherwise, she'll be the new albatross around all of our necks." Tess stood and dusted off her clothes. She walked across the patch of grass and retrieved her purse. "Go back. Tell her everything is all taken care of."

"And then what?" Nikki asked.

"Then we see what she does."

nineteen

CHARRIE WAS PLEASED with herself. Soon she would be queen of the castle. The bank accounts, the clients, the power—she deserved them all.

She stepped into her heels. She loved heels. They showed off her legs, one of her strongest features. Now she went to the mirror. For the past year, she'd looked at her reflection differently, searching for any similarity, some physical likeness to make a connection. Each time the mirror reflected back only the image she'd come to know. But even if her face didn't show the truth, documents didn't lie. Not like people.

She checked the mirror again, leaned closer, and applied more lipstick. She wanted to impress tonight's dinner guests. She'd make them forget all about Tess McDonald.

Over the years, she'd watched Tess charm man after man with no more than a slight touch or a mysterious smile. Oh, how she'd admired her boss. She admired Tess's style, her cool control, her ability to make anyone feel like the most important person in the world—even as she was plotting the next conquest.

Charrie fell for the same illusion herself. She'd believed that she was the most important person to Tess. But that was all a lie, part of the façade, one of many; like the belief that her parents were her own flesh and blood, but there was always something missing. Not until she finally looked in her parents' lockbox did she realize what that was.

The night they died, she'd been out with friends, partying. She was sixteen and it was Saturday night. When her cab pulled onto her street, Charrie saw the flashing lights of the fire trucks, and flames and smoke everywhere. Neighbors were out in the street in their pajamas, shaking their heads and pointing.

She jumped out of the cab, running and screaming toward the blaze that engulfed her home. A police officer leaped from the crowd and stopped her.

"My mom! My dad!"

He held her like a vise. "Stand back. There's nothing you can do. Let the fireman do their work."

She struggled against him. Her eyes searched the crowd. "Ma! Daddy!" she screamed until her throat was raw.

"Poor thing," she heard someone mutter behind her.

"Tragedy," said another.

It was nearly an hour before they were able to get the fire under control. Charrie sat on the curb across the street, held there by the same police officer who'd stopped her an hour ago. He had refused to leave her side. He'd put a blanket around her because even in the steamy summer night she shivered as if dipped in a bucket of ice.

She watched EMS bring out two black bags on a stretcher, and it was like looking at someone else's life.

"Is there anyone you can stay with tonight?" the officer asked gently.

She simply stared at the ruins of her house. Her next coherent thought was the following morning when she woke up in a shelter run by the Red Cross.

A social worker was standing over her when she opened her eyes. "I'm Mrs. Thomlinson, sweetheart. There are some clean clothes for you at the foot of the bed. The bathroom is at the end of the hall. Why don't you get up and get dressed so that we can talk."

She did as she was told, the images of the previous night clouding her vision.

When Charrie emerged from the bathroom, Mrs. Thomlinson was waiting. She put her arm around Charrie's shoulder and led her to an office on the other side of the building.

"I know you've undergone a traumatic loss. And I know it will be hard to deal with, but I'm here to help you."

Charrie stared blankly and rocked back and forth in the chair with her arms wrapped tightly around her body.

"Do you have any family that we can contact?"

She shook her head. She didn't know of any aunts, uncles, or grandparents. All she'd had was her mom and dad.

"How old are you, Charrie?"

"Sixteen."

The social worker wrote something down on a form and then stuck it in a folder and closed it. She folded her hands on the top of the desk. "For the time being, we will have to put you in a group home so that you can be looked after."

Charrie eyed her dully, trying to make sense of what the woman was saying.

"Hopefully we'll be able to find you suitable foster parents." The social worker paused. "I am so sorry for your loss," she said. "We'll do all we can to try to make it as easy as possible for you."

They never did find a suitable foster family. And no one wanted to adopt a teenager. So Charrie spent the next two years in Amber House for Girls. She finished school with relatively good grades and worked part-time at the gym, where she'd met Tess. Her dream had been to enter the field of journalism. But Tess had shown her another world.

Tess had become the mother Charrie desperately missed. She clung to the older woman, living for her every word and action.

Her own mother had been a plain woman, nothing fancy about her. She shopped at discount stores and bought her shoes from Payless. She did her own hair on Saturday nights and spent her Sundays in church. Her father was a laborer, pure blue collar. He owned one suit.

By contrast, the life that Tess showed her was filled with handsome, wealthy men, gorgeous clothes, trips, parties, and conversations about the wider world. Tess taught Charrie how to be the perfect hostess, how to wear clothes that enhanced her body, how to apply makeup to bring out her features. She instructed her on the art of conversation, how to walk and how to hold a man's attention with a simple look, command a room just by walking into it. She taught her about the power of femininity and how to wield that power.

Tess never allowed her to "entertain" the clients. She didn't

want that part of the life for Charrie. Instead she taught her protégée the intricacies of running an elite service, what to look for
in employees, and how to screen the male clients. After some
time, she could step into Tess's shoes effortlessly.

On her twenty-first birthday, Charrie received a call from her
deceased parents' attorney. Now that she was of age, he could
pass on the lockbox her parents left behind.

"Are you going to open it?" Tess asked as they were sitting together in Tess's posh penthouse apartment with a skyline view of
Manhattan.

Charrie held the metal box on her lap. She gripped the key in
her fist. "Opening it up won't bring them back," she said. "All it
will do is bring back memories I've been trying to forget." She
swallowed over the growing knot in her throat. "For months after
the fire I had nightmares," she said in a distant voice. "In some ver-
sions I'm home. I smell the smoke, wake my parents, and we get
out. In others I'm running and running to their bedroom, but the
more I run the farther away the room gets. And then there's
the real nightmare   me standing out on the street, helpless, as
the house goes up in flames." She sniffed and blinked rapidly. Her
lips were pressed tightly together.

Tess lowered her head and put her arm around Charrie's stiff
shoulders to draw her close. "Look," Tess said, her voice low
and soothing, "why don't we take this down to the bank and put
it in one of my safe deposit boxes. I'll give you a key. And whenever you're ready, you can go in and get it, but in the meantime,
the box won't be a constant reminder. How does that sound,
sweetie?"

Charrie ran her hand across the cool metal. She handed it to
Tess.

She hadn't gone to the bank to check on the contents for nearly seven years—until they'd received the anonymous call about the pending raid. Tess closed out all the accounts as well as the safe deposit boxes.

The lockbox had sat in her new apartment for nearly a month, on the top shelf of her closet. One Friday night after a hard day at work and several glasses of wine, Charrie felt brave enough to open it.

The box was filled with childhood photos, love letters between her parents, her old report cards, and immunization records. One by one, she relived each photograph, remembering the trips to the zoo, her first school play, graduation from junior high school. She lovingly touched the smiling faces of her parents. Instead of the pain she thought she would feel, she experienced a sense of peace—closure, of sorts.

At the bottom of the strongbox was a thick sealed envelope that had begun to yellow around the edges. She took the envelope out of the box, turning it over several times in her hand.

She put her glass of wine on the nightstand and opened the envelope. Inside it were folded sheets of paper. She unfolded the stack.

At first what she was seeing didn't make any sense to her. These were adoption papers. Her parents had adopted a child? She read on, and as she did, her insides tightened, her heart raced.

On January 28, 1979, Brenda and Charles Lewis adopted Baby Jane Doe.

She flipped through the legal documents and came upon a birth certificate for a baby girl born on November 12, 1978, to Tess McDonald, birth mother, father's name unknown. She read the certificate three times. It couldn't be right. The age of mother at time of birth—nineteen. Place of birth—George Washington University Hospital, Washington, D.C.

Her head began to pound. Tess McDonald gave birth to a baby girl on *her* birthday, November 12, 1978, and gave the baby up for adoption to Brenda and Charles Lewis. Her stomach lurched. Her mother always told her that she'd been born in GWU Hospital.

This couldn't be right. It simply couldn't. It was all some sort of bizarre coincidence. That had to be it. She searched through the papers, certain that something in them would explain the confusion. But what she came across was an official document wherein Tess McDonald severed all parental rights and freely gave her baby up for adoption. Her signature was there. . . . *Tess's signature* . . . a signature Charrie had committed to memory by now. She'd even practiced the stylish scrawl so often, she could get away with minor forgeries.

She looked at the smiling photographs that she'd spread out on the couch. *Liars.* Her "parents" had lied to her for years, pretending to be something they weren't. *Liars.* Her own life was a lie. The knowledge rocked her. Everything about her had been built on a lie. Her mother wasn't the president of the PTA. Her mother was a professional whore. A whore whose life of money and luxury was more important than the life of her child—conceived by a john, probably.

Her stomach rushed to her throat. She ran toward the bathroom but didn't make it. She retched and emptied and retched until there was nothing left but dry heaves.

She wasn't sure how long she'd sat huddled in her vomit at the bathroom door. But when she snapped out of her shock she vowed to ruin Tess and everything the woman held dear, just as Tess had ruined everything for her.

————

CHARRIE HAD ARRANGED a small dinner party for two gentleman who were visiting the villa from London. They'd been referred by a satisfied client. Nonetheless, she'd checked them out thoroughly before extending the invitation. One couldn't be too careful. This was to be her first in-person meeting with them.

She strolled into the living area, all smiles and grace. One of the women was chatting with them when she entered.

"I hope you've been given the tour of the house," Charrie said, gliding farther into the room. She extended her hand. "Thank you for keeping them company, Amina."

"Not a problem. I hope to see you both later." The young woman smiled and walked away.

The first man stood, his eyes gleaming with interest at the sight of Charrie. He took her hand. "Warren Lang," he said, his British accent clear and cool.

"My pleasure." She shook his hand. "Welcome." She turned to the second gentleman. "And you must be Mr. Fields." She turned on her hundred-watt smile.

"Please, call me Clarke."

Charrie nodded slightly.

A waitress she'd hired for the night brought out a plate of appetizers and stood holding it out to them.

Charrie took a seat and slowly crossed her long, polished legs, revealing a bit of thigh. "So, gentleman, how long do you plan to stay in Aruba?" She took a paté from the platter, excused the servant, and nibbled daintily.

She spent the next twenty minutes or so engaging them in light conversation, feeling them out, getting a sense of their wants. As she listened to them talk, she was deciding on which of her beautiful and talented ladies would be best suited for each client just as Kimberly and Nicole walked in.

Charrie glanced over her shoulder. As they approached, she tried to read their expressions. Had they done it? The pulse in her throat beat a little faster. They'd been gone all day. Was Tess finally an afterthought? But their eyes and their body language reflected only calm, style, and grace. They were both dressed for the occasion.

Nicole's exotic beauty was emphasized by the coral-colored cocktail dress that hugged her tiny waist and fanned out at the knee to showcase her shapely legs. Her waist-length hair was pulled up and twisted into a loose French knot. Gold drop earrings hung from her lobes. Her entire persona telegraphed hot passion.

Kimberly was just as striking but in a completely opposite manner. She was an object of sophistication. Her ensemble of sea blue matched the cool color of her eyes. Her blond hair was pulled back tightly from her face, emphasizing her sharp cheekbones. Her signature diamond studs dotted her ears and matched the bracelet on her right wrist.

"Good evening," Kimberly said. Her gaze took in everyone at once and instantly commanded the room.

Charrie felt that she had been almost imperceptibly pushed gently to the side.

Kimberly approached the guests. Both men stood as if pulled up by invisible strings.

"Clarke Fields."

"Warren Lang."

She shook each man's hand in turn. "Kimberly."

They turned their attention to Nicole, who approached with a wicked grin on her lush mouth.

"Nicole. But, please call me Nikki. All of my friends do."

They both flushed red.

Charrie cut in. "Kimberly and Nicole are my . . . business partners." She shot a glance at the women. "We were just getting acquainted. I was asking Clarke and Warren how we can help make their stay more enjoyable."

"I'm sure you'll have a wonderful time," Kim said.

"How long are you planning to stay in Aruba?" Nicole asked. She transferred a paté from the platter onto a small plate.

"About a week. We have business here, and then we go back to London."

"I see. What kind of business are you in?"

"We're in financing. We've been considering opening a hotel. The tourist market has jumped for this side of the world, and we want to be in on it," Clarke said.

From there, Kim controlled the conversation. Her years of experience in high-level negotiations made it an exchange that she mastered easily. She offered suggestions, discussed financing options, feeling truly energized for the first time in ages. This was who she really was; a businesswoman with a keen mind. A woman who had vision and ambition. She missed the boardroom, the day-to-day push to stay on top. She missed the power she once wielded.

"You're quite well versed," Warren said.

Kim smiled. "I try to stay on top of things." She stood abruptly. "It was a pleasure meeting both of you. I hope that your business and your pleasure are all that you're looking for."

"I'm sure it will be," Clarke said. Kim made a move to leave, but the businessman continued: "I'd really like to speak with you some more about your ideas."

Kim stopped short, not sure if he was sincere or simply offering a euphemism for getting her in bed as part of his "pleasure."

"I'm sure something can be arranged. Good night."

Charrie's jaw was clenched so tightly, her head began to throb. That bitch had taken over, charmed them, which was *her* job. It was what *she* did. Everyone else was simply accessories, there to make her *look* good.

Was this Tess's real reason for bringing them here, to eventually push her out? Charrie's rage brewed. She wouldn't sit still for it. No way in hell.

"We'll talk later?" she said sweetly to Nikki and Kim although her tight expression belied her tone.

"Yes We have a few things to discuss," Nikki said, giving her a pointed look.

Charrie nodded and then turned back to her guests. "Now, where were we?"

"YOU WERE DAMNED GOOD in there," Nikki said as she and Kim walked out back. "Got a lot of shit with you. Had me wanting to buy up some property." She chuckled.

Kim flinched at Nikki's language, although by now she should have grown accustomed to her partner's sailor mouth. She had to admit, however, that at least Nikki knew how to act in front of company—look pretty and keep her mouth shut.

"It's what I do," Kim said. "You can't build a thriving enterprise and not understand the dynamics of economics."

Nicole cut her eyes in Kimberly's direction. "Whatever."

"You have the story straight about what we're going to tell Charrie, right?"

"Yeah, I got it."

"If Tess knows her as well as she thinks, it's only a matter of time."

They walked out to the pool. The moonlight reflected off the still water. In the distance, the cry of night birds could be heard. It was the picture of tranquillity.

Kim stretched out on a lounge chair and kicked off her shoes. She closed her eyes and Clarke's face emerged. While she'd been talking with him, she found herself as taken by his knowledge as by his presence. He made her think of that actor Pierce Brosnan, with a little more weight to him—tall, dark, and wickedly handsome. His cool English bearing was as much a turn-on as the way his dark eyes glimmered in the light when he laughed.

How could she be having feelings for a man? In her marriage to Troy, the sex between them had gone from hot to superficial to duty-bound. Her true passion had been for Stephanie. Only with her had she truly experienced the rush of sexual fulfillment.

Yet, when Clarke held her hand . . .

"What's on your mind?" Nikki asked, interrupting her thoughts.

"Nothing," she said absently.

"Well, get on your A-game. Here comes Ms. Thing now."

TWENTY

"THIS HAS REALLY BEEN GREAT," Mark was saying as he and Tracy lay nestled together in bed. The flames from the bedroom fireplace snapped and crackled in the dark.

"Yes, it has," she said, surprised that she really meant it. She kissed his bare shoulder. "It's been a while since I've let someone get this close to me. I guess that's why I was a little distant and edgy at first."

"I understand. Relationships take time. But I'm willing to wait as long as it takes."

She turned around in his arms to face him. "Why?"

"Because you're important to me, Vicky. I believe we can have something special and good between us."

Even if I'm not who you think I am? She didn't respond aloud. She closed her eyes and rested her head against his chest. He'd opened up about his past, the things he'd done and endured to get to where he was now. She, on the other hand, couldn't offer him the same thing. She couldn't tell him that her name wasn't Victoria Styles, that she wasn't a widow, that she hadn't worked at a small law firm in New York.

That was the hardest part of her new life: the lies, keeping up the façade, remembering all the little details that had been woven together to create this new person she'd become, imagining one day that she would slip up and spill the beans or get caught in her own fabrication.

How could she ever hope to have a real life if the life she was living was all make-believe?

"Why the sigh?" he asked, stroking her shoulder.

She hadn't realized she'd done that. "Just content, I guess," she lied.

"Content is good." He turned her onto her back in one easy move. He looked down into her eyes. "I want you to know that you can trust me, Vicky. You can trust me with your hurts, your joys, your happiness. I wouldn't do anything to lose that trust." He pushed her legs apart with a gentle sweep of his thighs. "I'm in love with you. And with a little time . . ."

She felt him grow hard against her, and her body immediately became warm and fluid.

". . . and a little effort . . ." He lifted her legs over the bend in his arms. He pushed against her opening, sliding in and filling her.

Her breath caught. Her hips rose to meet him.

"I know you will feel the same way. . . ."

Maybe she could, she thought as she wrapped her legs around his waist and ground her pelvis against his thrusts. Mark groaned in her ear, and a shiver of delight raced through her. Maybe she could risk being in love and giving it in return. Mark was everything that a woman wanted in a man, and he wanted *her*—or at least the woman he thought he knew.

Was that enough?

"Is it possible that sex gets better between us each time?" Mark said, his face pointed toward the ceiling.

Tracy breathed heavily. Her body still tingled all over. "If it is possible, we must be going for a record." She giggled and pulled the sheet up to her waist.

"I'm all for it."

His pager went off, vibrating along the nightstand. He leaned over and peered at the number. When his pager went off and he was off-duty it could only be trouble.

"It's the station," he said, turning to look at her. He sat up and tossed off the sheet. "Need to use your phone."

"Sure." She sat up as well, pressing her hand to his back as he dialed.

"I'll be right there."

He hung up. "Fire out of control downtown. It's already gone to two alarms. They anticipate three," he was saying as he hunted the room for his clothes. "Commercial strip with some apartments above." He tugged his shirt over his head. "Those are the worst." Tracy handed him his shorts and pants.

Before she knew it, he was at the door, stepping into his boots and putting on his coat. "Be back as soon as I can."

"Take care of yourself."

"I will." He kissed her gently. "You, too." He winked and then darted for his SUV.

Tracy closed the door slowly behind him, a soft smile on her mouth. *My man off to do his thing.* Maybe it would be all right. She tightened the belt on her robe then went back upstairs to straighten the bedroom. The sheets were damp and twisted into knots. She wanted things to be nice for him when he got back. He'd be exhausted and would need a good night's sleep.

She changed the linens, took a shower, then went down to fix something to eat. It wasn't long before she grew bored of surfing through the television channels and her mind went back into ADA mode. The files that she'd begun paging through seemed to be calling her. She got up from the couch and retrieved the names and phone numbers that she'd set aside. Nicole Perez's probation officer might still be at work. She dialed, and after several rings, Officer Nita Williams picked up.

Tracy identified herself as a liaison with the DA office, giving a clearance code but not her name. She provided pertinent information on the case, information that only someone with authority would have.

"Okay, so you're working with the DA's office. How can I help you?"

"I need to find out what contacts, appointments, et cetera, were made upon Nicole Perez's release."

"Hold on."

Tracy waited and listened patiently to all the background noises, cusses, and paper shuffling. Finally Officer Williams got back on the line.

"Okay, let's see. She was released, and her last known address was in East Harlem with her brother Ricky. If I remember correctly, he picked her up and brought her down to see me a couple of times. She'd had a pretty rough time of it in prison. Some of the women roughed her up pretty bad, if you know what I mean."

Tracy cringed.

"I made an appointment with . . . hmmm, let's see . . . a doctor Annette Hutchinson. Pretty classy place, private office, figured that would make Nikki feel good, ya know, not some clinic."

Tracy wrote down the name, which sounded very familiar. "Uh, what kind of doctor is Hutchinson?"

"Ob/gyn. She needed looking after, know what I mean?"

Annette Hutchinson. The name definitely rang a bell. "Anything else?"

"That's pretty much it. I only had minimal contact for the first three months. She'd done her full bid. I was only a resource. Oh, there was one thing, the same day I'd made the appointment for Nikki wound up being the same day as that massive East Coast blackout." She chuckled. "Figures, right? Anyway, when I'd asked her about it, she said she was there but had to reschedule. Not sure if she ever went back."

"Thanks. Do you have a phone number or address for Hutchinson?"

"Yeah, here ya go." She read off the information.

"Thanks. You've been a big help."

"Is Nikki in trouble?"

"No. Just doing some follow-up."

"Yeah, that's what you all say. Good luck." She hung up the phone.

Tracy hung up, too. Where had she heard that name before? Hutchinson, Hutchinson, Hutchinson . . . Then it hit her.

One day, years earlier when a temporary truce had been struck between her and Tess, they were having lunch at an outdoor café in Midtown Manhattan. Tracy hadn't been able to eat much and mentioned to Tess about her irregular cycle. Tess quickly suggested an Annette Hutchinson.

"She's the best," Tess said. "I've used her for years and recommend her to anyone that will listen." She'd fished in her bag and pulled out a card, then handed it to Tracy. "She's really good." She nodded as she spoke. "And you'll like her."

Tess and Nikki had used the same doctor. Is that where they'd met, where the connection had been made?

Her heart started to race. She jumped from the couch and began to pace. Her mind churned with possibilities. She'd briefly spoken to her sister the day after the blackout. She didn't mention that she'd been to the doctor—not that she would have. But it was possible. Either that or they'd met when Nikki rescheduled.

What about Kim Benning? She checked the address of Dr. Hutchinson's office. Uptown. Classy, pricey. Just the kind of place that the high-caliber Kimberly Shepherd-Benning would visit.

Was that the connecting link—Dr. Hutchinson's office? She felt so close to uncovering yet another layer, she could almost taste success.

She paced back and forth in front of the television and caught a glimpse of the news. The correspondent was on location. Behind him a complete block was ablaze. At first she thought it was another report on the war until she noticed the caption beneath: MONTAUK STREET, COLORADO SPRINGS. She grabbed the remote and turned up the volume.

"As you can see behind me, almost the entire block is on fire. Fire Chief Grisham said that the fire surged out of control moments after the arrival of the first unit. This street is both residential and commercial, which makes fighting the fire that much more dangerous. Several of these buildings—a computer repair shop and a hardware store—are filled with combustible materials, which, according to sources, are feeding the blaze. There've been reports of injuries. We're not sure yet if they were civilians or firemen."

An explosion ripped behind him. Debris shot into the air. He jumped and turned. The roofs on two of the buildings collapsed, taking at least four firefighters with them.

Tracy gasped and moved closer to the television.

The correspondent was pressing his hand to his earpiece. "It seems that three, maybe four firefighters fell when the roof collapsed," he was saying. "With the thick smoke and the instability of the buildings, it will be difficult to get them out."

"Oh my God," Tracy whispered. She moved backwards until her legs met the couch; slowly she sat down, transfixed by the scene in front of her.

"Is the weather having an impact, as well, Jay?" the anchor in the station asked on a split screen.

"Absolutely, Tara. The winds are feeding the flames, and the icy temperatures are freezing the water as fast as it settles."

"Thanks, Jay. That was Jay Dennis on location. We'll keep you up to date on this event as more details become available. This is Tara Warner, News Twelve. We'll be back after this commercial break."

Tracy had her fist pressed to her mouth during the final moments of the newscast. Of course Mark was fine. There was no reason to worry. By the time the fire was put out and everything settled, he'd call. She was sure of it.

Suddenly the files, finding connections, and pointing fingers of guilt didn't mean a damn thing.

She waited for a call that never came. Not that night and not until the next afternoon. It was from the captain of his battalion.

"Is this Victoria Styles?"

"Yes." She said a silent prayer.

"This is Captain Donahue from Engine Company Four. I wanted to tell you about Mark."

She held her breath.

"He's in the hospital. He's . . . in pretty bad shape."

He was alive. Thank God. "Can I see him?"

"Right now he's in intensive care at Mary Mount Hospital. They aren't allowing any visitors. But I'm pretty sure I can get you in." He paused. "Mark talked about you all the time."

Tears suddenly sprang to her eyes, and her throat burned. "Th-thank you."

"I'll give you a call back as soon as I get approval. I just can't guarantee that it will be today. Gotta see what the docs are saying."

"I understand."

"A bunch of the guys are hanging out here at the hospital, waiting for word on Mark and a couple of others. I could have someone come and pick you up. . . ."

"Thank you. I'd appreciate that." She knew she was in no shape to concentrate on driving in this weather.

"Give the driver about an hour. The roads are a bitch. 'Scuse my French."

Tracy sniffed and smiled. "Sure." She barely noticed when she hung up the phone.

He's alive, she continued to repeat to herself. That was what was important. All the rest . . . She didn't want to think about it. She ran upstairs to get dressed and wait.

TWENTY-ONE

CHARRIE APPROACHED THEM, her expression resolute. "Nice show you put on in there," Charrie said to Kim.

Kim didn't respond.

"Well, what happened? Is everything taken care of?"

"Let's put it this way," Nicole said, "you won't ever have to worry about Tess McDonald again. As they say in the movies, she sleeps with the fishes."

Charrie's features pinched for an instant. She quickly regained her composure. "Good. With Tess . . . out of the way, the business and all that goes with it are ours."

Nicole stared at her hard. "You're a cold bitch. You didn't even flinch, and this was a woman that you've been with for ten years. No honor among thieves," she muttered. "Makes me wonder what you would do to us."

"Hopefully none of us will have to worry about that." She turned smartly and walked away.

"Real piece of work," Nicole murmured.

"I think she may have met her match this time," Kim said.

"Yeah, if Tess is as good as her game, it's only a matter of time."

CHARRIE WENT TO HER ROOM. She shut the door and then pressed her back against it. An array of emotions swirled through her: satisfaction, vindication, joy, and an incomprehensible sorrow.

Tess, gone. Dead. Her body mere pieces at the bottom of the ocean. Her chest tightened until she began gasping for air. She stumbled to the bathroom and splashed cold water on her face. Gripping the edge of the sink for support, she glanced up into the mirror.

What have I done?

Maybe there could have been some other way. Maybe she should have confronted Tess with her knowledge long ago instead of selling herself to that devil in a blue suit—Avery Powell. Maybe Tess could have offered an explanation. Now Charrie would never know.

She'd been consumed by her rage and sense of betrayal, blinded to anything other than revenge. She turned away from her image in the glass, reached for a towel, and dried her face.

It was done, she reasoned. There was no turning back now; it was no time to get soft and nonvigilant. She had to be more cautious now than ever before. And if there was one thing that Tess taught her, it was never to leave loose ends. Kim and Nicole were loose ends, and they had to go.

Charrie went to the bed and sat down. She opened a drawer

and took out a brown leather book that had a lock on it. The key to the lock stayed with her at all times. In the book were all the important contact numbers. She removed the tiny gold key from inside her bra and opened the book. She flipped through the pages until she found Winston Sinclair's phone number.

He would want to know what those wicked women had confessed to her about what they'd done. She knew Winston had a special place in his heart for Tess, and as prime minister of the island, nothing was out of his reach.

VINCENT WAS BEYOND LIVID. "I told you to let me go with you. I should have gone with my instincts and followed you." He glared at her. "You could have been killed!"

Tess tightened the belt around her robe and ran a towel through her damp hair. "But I'm not dead. They didn't kill me, and I convinced them that the only way to get to Charrie was to turn the tables on her."

Vincent grabbed her shoulders so hard, she yelped. "What if you hadn't? What if those crazy women had tossed you over the fucking cliff? Christ!" He squeezed her to him tightly, and she couldn't breathe. "After all the shit I've been through, after all we've been through, I'm not going to lose you now, Tess."

"You will if you don't let me go. I can't get air."

Reluctantly he released her. "I should kill you myself for making me go crazy all day."

"Baby—" She stroked the hard line of his jaw. "—I'm here, you're here. That's all that matters. The rest will take care of itself."

"Don't try to pacify me. I'm still pissed," he said, with a little less fire in his voice.

"It's my job to pacify you." She gave him a dark look and un-fastened the belt on her robe. She shrugged her shoulders and let the robe fall to the floor.

Vincent's eyes feasted on her body, still damp and dewy from her shower. "Don't try to distract me," he said, reaching out to cup the weight of her breast in his palm. He ran his thumb across a taut nipple.

She arched her neck slightly. "I won't." She began unfastening the buttons of his shirt. "I'll just keep you completely occupied." She tugged his shirt down his arms, then tossed it aside. When he reached for her, she pushed his hands away and undid his belt then his zipper.

"Let's do this my way, hmmm?" she said, reaching up to nibble at his ear, while she gently stroked his bulging shaft.

"Kinda hard to protest when you have me at such a disadvan-tage."

She wound her way down his body, taking his pants with her until they pooled at his feet. She looked up, and he was staring down at her, his cock at full staff. She licked the underside, and he sucked in his breath. She did it again and again, watching it jump and throb.

Her tongue danced around the tip, and she felt his thighs tremble.

He grabbed the back of her head. "Take it," he urged in a ragged voice.

"All in good time," she whispered, licking a single drop of liquid.

He hissed between his teeth. Slowly she stood up, holding him in her palm, stroking him up and down. She guided him toward the bed and pushed him down onto his back. She stood over him, her eyes like hot coals trailing across his body.

Damn, he was gorgeous. Vincent Royal was what would be considered a beautiful specimen of a man. His abs rippled, like they'd been cut from granite. His thighs were thick and hard. His chest was broad and his arms bulged with sculpted muscle. Vincent was handsome by any measure. Emitting a raw sexual energy, Vincent was a man that could make you lose your mind. She certainly had. She'd let Vincent have more of her than just her body, Tess thought as she took a cock ring out of her purse.

Vincent's eyes darkened. "And what do you plan to do with that?"

She straddled him. "Take you to heaven and me right along with you," she whispered, sliding it along his length until it reached the hilt.

"Ahhh," he groaned, shutting his eyes against the sudden intense pleasure. "What else do you have in your little black bag, Doctor?" he asked, his voice thick.

She grinned, leaned over, and reached inside it. She took out something small and silver and clipped it to her clit. She moaned softly before raising herself up. She positioned his shaft right at her wet opening and slowly rotated her hips but wouldn't let him in. Each time he surged upward, she pulled back to intensify the short bursts of contact between them.

Unable to hold back, Vincent grabbed her hips and pushed her all the way down on him.

Tess cried out, arched all the way back until her head was nearly between his knees.

He slid his finger between their bodies and rubbed the ring on her clit. She hollered in delight and rolled her hips even harder. He kept up the pressure, feeling her juices spill over his fingertips.

Tess jerked upward and rode him straight up and down, her

breasts bouncing wildly, her damp hair swinging around her face as one wave of release after another ripped through her.

Vincent flipped her onto her back, never losing the connection, and buried himself even deeper inside her.

Tess reached up between his legs and massaged his sac as they moved in perfect harmony with each other.

His cock had grown so hard and so large from the ring, he was sure it would split if he didn't get relief. Yet at the same time he didn't want it to end. His head spun.

Tess's slender fingers found the ring fastened at the base of his shaft and slowly slid it toward the tip. Vincent began to groan. His body stiffened. She widened her legs, grabbed the pillow from beneath her head, and shoved it under her hips.

Vincent exploded, pounding into her, as the ejaculation took on a life of its own. He thought it would never stop—the tremors, the electricity, the ecstasy. He came and came until there was nothing left and all his weight collapsed on her.

Tess tenderly wrapped her arms around him and held him close.

"Is that your plan every time we have a disagreement?" Vincent asked once they'd finally caught their breaths.

Tess giggled. "Of course."

Vincent shook his head. "Guess I don't stand a chance of winning any arguments."

"Depends. Maybe you can get a little black bag of your own."

He turned his head to look at her. She was grinning.

"I'll take you toy shopping one day, let you pick out a few things," she offered.

"At least I'd be on the same playing field." He stroked her thigh. There were times when he was making love to Tess that he wondered if the things she did to and with him were the same as her moves with other men. Was it all part of a game, or was it real to her? "I need to know something."

"What?"

"What makes this different for you?"

"I don't know what you mean." But even as she said it, she knew where this conversation was heading. She'd known it would come sooner or later.

He thought about the best way to put it. "I know that you've been with other men. And I know that part of what you did was . . . to make them happy." He saw her expression tense, but he continued. "What separates what we do from what you did for money?"

"I learned a long time ago that the housewife isn't much different from the whore." She stared him in the eyes. "Housewives fuck their husbands for kids, for an allowance, to keep them happy, because the Bible tells them to, for the new house or a new car. Girlfriends screw their boyfriends in the hopes of a big wedding day, nice dinners, and a trip to the mall. Whores fuck for two reasons: pleasure and money. The bottom line is women fuck men for a variety of reasons. They give something and expect to get something in return. Whores are no different from women who screw men they don't love. But whores are very clear about the reasons why they fuck. And men know the reasons going in. They aren't deluded."

"So, this is just another fuck for you, is that what you're saying?" He pushed up on his elbows.

"Every now and again, something slips past all that material gain." She swallowed. "Every now and then two people really feel something for each other, and they stop fucking and make love." She looked into his eyes. "Even us whores. And we do it because we want to, and we want that man to know we want to make them happy." She stroked his cheek. "I want to make you happy, Vince. Because when you are, I know I will be. And happiness is something I've been looking for all my life."

He shifted onto his side. His gaze dragged over her face. "I'm sorry. That was an ugly question, but I needed to know."

"I was wondering what took you so long."

"We all have baggage. We all have a past."

"Yeah, 'cept some folks' bags are heavier than others."

He rolled onto his back and laughed. "You got that right."

Tess folded her hands across her stomach. "What do you think Charrie's next move will be?"

"I don't know. But this time out, we're going to do things my way."

She slanted a look in his direction.

He pointed a finger at her. "And no *buts* from you." He tossed off the sheet and got out of bed.

"Where are you going?"

"Tell you all about it when I get back. Stay put." He went to the bathroom.

She tossed her head back against the pillow and listened to the shower turn on. Hmmm, it was kind of nice having a man take charge of things for a change. She tucked her hands behind her head. Maybe this love thing wouldn't be so bad after all. She glanced toward the closed bathroom door. She still wanted to know what he was planning to do.

Tess got out of bed and padded into the bathroom. She pushed open the sliding glass door and stepped under the water. If he wouldn't tell her outright, perhaps she could convince him another way.

————

"YOU COULD BE OUT THERE for hours, days," Tess protested even as Vincent put on his clothes.

"True. But the longer I stay here debating the point with you, the more time I'm wasting."

"At least let me call Kim."

"No. The less everyone knows, the better." He cupped her chin in his palm. "I've done this a million times." The corner of his mouth quirked in a short grin. "I let you do what you do best, so let me do my thing. Okay?"

She sighed, defeated. "Fine. Go. Have it your way. I still think I should come with you."

"Forget it." He went for the door. "Besides, you'd be too much of a distraction."

"Let me call Kim," she pleaded one last time. "At least she could be a lookout."

"Fine," he relented, then wagged a finger at her, "but you stay put." He winked and walked out.

Tess plopped down on the edge of the bed after making her call. She should have been honest with Vincent—at least told him her suspicions. A chilling reality had been eating at her for days as she tried to come up with some logical reason for Charrie's sudden betrayal.

She'd gone over every single incident, conversation, confession, and meal she and Charrie had shared over the years. Most of all, she examined her feelings. She'd always questioned why she was so taken with the young girl she'd met at the spa, what it was that clicked between them. She attributed it to simple compatibility.

It wasn't until they'd come to Aruba that her unconscious feelings began to emerge. Still, it was only her speculation—a one-in-a-million chance.

She wasn't a praying woman. But if she were, she'd pray that she was wrong.

VINCENT SLOWED THE CAR. The villa was ahead. There was only one road in and out. He couldn't park on the property, and he couldn't very well sit out on the road. He'd been reluctant to take any assistance from Tess, but now he was glad that she'd insisted on contacting Kim. Kim would call Tess the moment Charrie left the villa.

At least now, if Charrie left the house, he would know which car to be on the lookout for. He pulled the car off to the side behind some shrubbery and under the shade of an enormous tree. At night he would blend right in. In the daytime, it would simply look like a car had stalled and was waiting for repairs.

He cut the engine, reclined the seat, and waited.He didn't even have time to get into a good position before his cell phone chirped.

"She's leaving now. She's in the black Benz."

"Thanks, babe."

"Vincent . . ."

"Yeah." He adjusted his seat and peered out into the darkness. He saw headlights approaching.

"Please, don't do anything . . . to hurt her."

"Relax." He disconnected the call. The car drove right past him. He gave her some time, started the engine, and went after her.

With the one road, it wasn't unusual to have a car behind you, so he wasn't concerned about Charrie wondering if she was being followed. Whenever she stopped, he would keep going and pull off somewhere then backtrack on foot if necessary. Hopefully she was doing more than running to the market for eggs.

He kept a reasonable distance, not too fast, not too slow. She made a turn at the fork in the road. Damn it. He had to keep going. When he was able to stop up ahead, he took a good look at his surroundings. This was where he'd been the night the doc drugged him. The prime minister's place was down the road that Charrie had turned onto.

How was Winston Sinclair involved?

TWENTY-TWO

THE DRIVE TO THE HOSPITAL seemed to last forever. Derek, Mark's coworker, tried to ease her tension as much as possible with small talk and non-funny jokes. She appreciated his effort.

"Mark's a tough guy. I'm sure he'll be fine."

"Do you know what happened exactly?"

"Well, I don't know how much of this I should say, but most of it's been on the news already. So I guess it's okay. There was basically no way we could fight the fire from the front, and we needed to make sure it didn't spread to the block behind us. . . ."

He went on to explain how Mark and three other members of the crew volunteered to go up on the roof. They needed to get water directly onto the blaze before it turned to ice. No one really knew how badly damaged the structures had become. The roof gave way, and they tumbled down inside.

"They were pinned in there for a good half hour before we could get to them. Then we had to dig through burning debris to find them."

Tracy held up her hand. She'd heard enough.

"I've seen guys pull through worse. The most important thing for recovery is having friends and family around for support. Ya know." He bobbed his head. "From what Mark's been telling me, you're the closest thing to family he has."

Her chest constricted. "He said that?"

"Yeah." He grinned. "You're pretty important to him. I been around Mark for a good five years now, and I've never really heard him talk about anyone else until you."

"Thank you for telling me that," she said softly.

They arrived at the hospital and went straight to the waiting room. It was filled with firefighters, some in their gear and others in their street clothes.

Derek ushered her over to the assemblage. "Guys, this is Mark's lady, Victoria. Victoria, these are the guys."

There were rounds of deep hellos and smiles.

The captain approached her. "I talked to the doctors. They said he's stable. He's still in ICU, but they may let him have a visitor in a couple of hours."

A sigh of relief rushed from her chest. "What are his injuries?"

He took her to the side. "He has a concussion, a couple of broken ribs, his right lung is punctured, and he had a broken leg. The biggest thing is the smoke that he gulped down. They have him on oxygen and a tube down his throat to help him breathe. So I know it won't be pretty when you see him."

She nodded tightly.

"You okay?"

"Yes," she whispered.

"You're just as pretty as Mark said you were."

She looked into his green eyes, which were filled with compassion and sincerity. "Thank you."

"Why don't you have a seat. It might be a while."

Two of the guys slid over on the plastic bench to let her sit. From there she counted the minutes and took the time to think.

She could picture Mark's smiling face and hear his laughter. He'd come into her life like a spring breeze, gentle and easy. She remembered the day they met: She'd been doing her grocery shopping and was carrying two armloads of groceries to the car when one of them burst open, spilling all the contents onto the street. As she bent down to salvage what she could, the next thing she knew a man was kneeling beside her. He'd been at the supermarket with some of the crew from the firehouse. He'd helped her to her car, introduced himself, and told her he'd been happy to rescue her and would love to do it again. He asked for her number.

She'd been reluctant to give it to him at first, but then he told her that his buddies would vouch for him. He'd turned to his partners behind him, and they all gave grins and thumbs-up. She'd relented and wrote down her number. And it seemed from then on he'd been a fixture in her life. His presence had grown slowly with each passing day.

But it wasn't until last night that she realized how important he'd become to her. Her world seemed to come to a grinding halt when she heard about the fire and then received the call confirming her fears.

He'll be all right, she told herself again. And the first chance she got, she was going to tell him just how much he meant to her.

Someone was tapping her on the shoulder. She opened her eyes, not realizing that she'd dozed off.

The captain was standing over her. "The doc said you can see him for a few minutes."

She got up, draped her coat over her arm, and followed the captain down the long sterile corridor to the nurses' station.

"I'll leave you in Nurse Johnson's capable hands," the captain said.

"You'll have to leave your belongings out here and put on this gown over your clothing," the nurse told her. "You'll need to cover your head as well and put on gloves."

Nurse Johnson handed her the items and took her bag and coat. Then she handed Tracy paper slippers. "Your shoes, too." She put everything into a large clear plastic bag. "The area is completely sterile," she said as she led Tracy down the hall. The gown is to protect the patients. Burn victims are very susceptible to infection."

Burn patients. My God, they hadn't told her about that.

"Fortunately for your friend, his burns are not as bad as some others."

She swallowed. "How . . . bad?"

"Second- and some third-degree on his legs." She pushed through a swinging door then continued down the hall. She stopped in front of a glass door and turned to Tracy. "You can stay only five minutes. If he wakes up, don't try to make him talk."

Tracy nodded.

The nurse pushed the door open and stepped inside, with Tracy behind her. She went up to the bed and checked the machines whose humming filled the room. Satisfied, she turned to Tracy. "Five minutes. I'll be back for you."

"Thank you."

Hesitantly Tracy approached, and her heart lurched in her chest. His head was bandaged, his eyes were swollen to slits, and his face was bruised as if he'd been in a bar fight. A plastic tube was in his mouth and taped in place.

Mark's right leg was hoisted up at a forty-five-degree angle and held steady by pulleys. His hands were bandaged, and he was encased in a plastic bubble.

She felt like weeping but feared that he might open his eyes and see her tears. Slowly she drew closer, holding her breath. She covered her mouth to hold back a sob that leapt to her throat. She couldn't imagine from looking at him that he would ever be the same again.

"It looks a lot worse than it is," the nurse said from behind her. "What you see is superficial. His bruises and burns will heal and so will the broken bones. The major concern is his lungs. They were singed by the smoke and fire. But overall, he'll be fine." She patted Tracy's shoulder, and that's when the tears rolled down her cheeks and wouldn't stop.

"I'm sorry," she mumbled, and swiped at her eyes. "I . . ."

"It's okay. He's one of the lucky ones. A lot of them come in here and never make it home. It will take some time, but I'm sure he'll be fine."

Tracy blinked and blinked, trying to clear her vision. "Thank you." She looked at Mark one more time before leaving.

When she got back to the nurses' station, the captain was waiting for her as promised. Without a word, she stripped out of hospital attire, retrieved her belongings, and walked back to the waiting room with him.

"He's lucky," the captain said.

"That's what the nurse said. He doesn't look lucky."

"It's always hard to see someone you care about hurt or in pain. But he's going to get the best care in this hospital, and he'll be home before you know it."

She looked up at him, struggling to regain some semblance of composure. "Would it be okay if someone drove me home?"

"Sure. Not a problem."

THROUGHOUT THE NIGHT, Tracy tossed and turned. Several times she jumped up out of her sleep, thinking that she heard Mark calling her.

Shortly before daybreak she finally drifted into deep sleep. Her last conscious thoughts were of how unpredictable life was and how important it was to live for the moment and simply be happy. It was so easy to get caught up in all the things that, at the end of the day, didn't matter.

She wanted a life that mattered, a life in which *she* mattered. And she was going to make that happen. But first, there were some things she had to take care of.

TWENTY-THREE

CHARLIE WAITED in the receiving room of the prime minister's estate. She'd been here only once, when Tess introduced her to the PM upon their arrival. Of course, she'd made his acquaintance many more times afterwards at the villa, and that familiarity gave her the confidence that he would be more than willing to see her at this late hour.

She'd rehearsed her lines all evening. It was imperative that she be convincing if she wanted to tie off the last loose ends. Getting up from the plush love seat, she wandered over to the window that spanned one wall and looked out onto immaculate gardens. She swore she saw movement just outside the gates, and stepped closer. The movement stopped. Probably one of the groundskeepers or the swaying shadows from the trees, she decided.

"Charrie, to what do I owe the pleasure?"

She turned as Winston walked into the room.

He had a broad smile on his face. The prime minister came up to her and kissed her lightly on the cheek. "Earl said it was important." He'd had his fill of late-night visitors, he thought; hopefully this one would be pleasant and brief.

Charrie's eyes suddenly filled; her nostrils flared as though she were trying not to cry.

"Charrie!" He clasped her shoulder and looked down into her stricken face. "What is it?"

"I . . . I don't know how to tell you this." Her shoulders heaved. Winston ushered her over to the couch to sit down.

"Whatever it is, you can tell me." He reached for a carafe of water on the side table, but she waved it away.

Her head jerked up, and she looked into his eyes. "Tess is dead."

All the air rushed out of his lungs. He felt as if a sledgehammer had slammed into his gut, and he physically recoiled. "What happened? An accident?"

She pressed her hands against his. "No. It was no accident." She looked around frantically. "I'm so afraid. Are you sure no one can hear us?"

"Yes, yes," he rushed to say, needing to hear the details. "Tell me how you know this."

Charrie drew in a long breath, to pull herself together. "I was coming down the hallway this afternoon, and I heard hushed voices coming from one of the bedrooms. I guess they didn't realize the door was cracked." She lowered her head. "I shouldn't have listened, but I'm glad I did." She stared at him with defiance in her eyes.

Winston wanted to shake her into telling him what had happened to his Tess.

"I overheard Kim and Nicole talking about how they'd pushed Tess over the cliff out on Shadow Point."

Winston's warm brown face froze. The image of that cliff and the rocky waters below flashed in his head.

"They said that since Tess had already been gone a few days and everyone thought she was out of town . . ." She let her sentence drift off.

Dazed, he slowly pushed himself to a standing position. He tried to recall everything Tess said the last time he'd seen her. He knew she was in trouble, but he had no idea . . .

"They were laughing," Charrie added for effect, and watched Winston flinch. "They said that now with Tess out of the way, it was only a matter of time before the business would be theirs." She waited to see if he comprehended her innuendo.

He turned to her and saw the fear in her eyes.

"I didn't know where else to go, who to turn to. I couldn't go to the police."

Winston paced, his hand rubbing his chin. "Of course," he said absently. "You did the right thing by coming here."

"What are we going to do? They killed Tess. My God." She covered her face with her hands and wept.

Winston couldn't pull himself together to comfort her. He felt as if a part of him had died right along with Tess. How could this be? Not Tess.

"Did anyone see you come here?"

She looked up at him, her face tear-streaked. She shook her head.

"Good. I need you to go back to the house."

She jumped up and ran to him. "I can't." She grabbed the lapels of his jacket. "They'll kill me, too. I know it!" Her eyes widened.

He took her hands and put them down at her sides. "Go back to the house. They wouldn't try anything at the house, too many people in and out. If you don't go back, they'll know something is wrong. I'll take care of everything. Wait for my call."

Charrie sniffed hard and wiped her eyes. "All right." She started to move away. "You'll call, won't you?" she asked, sounding like a terrified child.

"I'll call."

She took her purse. Winston walked her to the door.

"Don't say anything to anyone. And don't let on that you know anything. Do you understand?" he pressed.

"I understand. I won't say a thing."

He opened the door and she stepped out. She turned to him. "Thank you," she whispered, then ran to her car.

Winston closed the door. His legs felt weak. He made it to the couch and crumpled. Not Tess.

He knew the kind of woman Tess was when he'd met her all those years ago, but that didn't matter. Somehow he saw beyond what she did to who she was. He'd loved her, and a part of him still did. But his position and his marriage had always been more important than his emotions. So he'd left her and tried to forget about her until one day she appeared on his doorstep. She was back in his life again, and he'd thrown caution to the wind to protect her and her business just so that she could be part of his existence, even in some small way.

By degrees, shock was replaced with grief and regret, and those replaced by a need for revenge. He'd never had a chance to tell her how he felt. But he could make them pay for what they'd done. That was how he would tell her.

VINCENT SAW HEADLIGHTS approach and then Charrie's car. For a moment he debated whether to follow her or go to the prime minister's house. Why had she come here? He decided on the second option. The difficulty would be getting on the other side of the gates. Well, he wasn't as young as he used to be, but he could still scale a ten-foot fence. Hopefully, it wasn't rigged with alarms.

He pocketed his car keys, checked his gun, and walked up the slope to the gate. Once up close, he realized that it wouldn't be so simple as he'd thought. He looked around for a way to gain some leverage.

On either side of the black steel gate was a granite wall that rose to meet the top of the gate. At least he'd be able to get some kind of grip; then of course, it was a drop down on the other side.

After a few false starts, he got a grip and made the slow, slippery ascent up the wall. His side was on fire. When he finally reached the top, the drop looked a hell of a lot steeper than the climb up.

It was either sit there or jump. If he was lucky, he wouldn't break anything. It was grass and dirt below, thankfully, and not concrete. He braced his body for the jump. His ankles and knees took the brunt of the fall before he twisted over onto his good side. He lay there for a moment, checking his body for injuries. Nothing was broken, and he didn't feel too much worse than he had before the fall.

He pulled himself up, dusted off his clothes, and started for the door with only a minor limp from his right ankle. He wouldn't be doing the marathon any time soon.

Vincent made it up to the front of the house without setting off any alarms. What he hadn't figured out was just what he was going to tell Winston. He knew that Tess trusted Winston, trusted him enough to bring him there when he'd been shot. Perhaps he would trust Vincent, as well. That's what he was banking on, anyway.

He got to the front door. The lights on the lower level were still on. Through the sheer drapes he could make out a figure pacing the room. It was Winston, and he was alone. Rather than alert the entire household to his presence, Vincent went to the window and tapped it.

Winston stopped for a moment and looked around. Vincent tapped again. Winston inched toward the window, his expression tight and cautious. He threw back the curtain. It took him several moments to recognize Vincent. His face contorted in rage.

He stormed to the door and flung it open. "Get away from my house before I call the police!"

"Wait, you don't want to do that. We need to talk."

Winston spun away. "I'm calling them now."

Vincent rushed in behind him, ran up on Winston, and grabbed him by the shoulders, whirled him around. "We need to talk. I want to know what Charrie was doing here. What she said to you."

"You've lost your mind." He opened his mouth to yell for help.

Vincent whipped his gun out and pointed it in Winston's gut. He clicked off the safety. "Don't even think about it."

Winston's nostrils flared.

"Now, close the door and have a seat."

Winston kept his eyes on Vincent as he did what he was told. He sat on the far side of the room, never taking his eyes off the gun.

"Good. Now we can talk like civilized gentlemen."

"You've been nothing but trouble since you arrived," he said, barely containing his rage. "You're probably involved in Tess's murder."

Vincent ran a hand over his face. "Tess isn't dead." Far from it, he thought, recalling the show she'd put on for him only hours earlier.

"You don't know what you're talking about. Those two women took her to the . . ." He couldn't finish.

Vincent went into his pocket and pulled out his cell phone. He pressed in the numbers. Tess answered on the second ring.

"There's someone who needs to speak with you." He handed Winston the phone.

Cautiously Winston took the phone and put it to his ear.

His eyes widened as he listened. "Yes . . . of course . . . thank God . . . I'll do whatever . . ." He disconnected the call and looked sheepishly up at Vincent. "I don't understand any of this. She said to trust you."

"And I knew if Tess trusted you, then so could I. That's why I came here after I saw Charrie leave."

Vincent put away the gun. He walked and talked, laying out as much of what he knew about the series of twisted events.

Winston was incredulous. "She did all of that simply to run the business?" He shook his head. "Does she resent Tess that much?"

"There's no other explanation we could come up with. But I'm sure she came here banking on the fact that once she told you what they'd allegedly done to Tess, you would take matters into your own hands and do her dirty work for her by making Nicole and Kim . . . disappear. I'm sure Charrie knew that you would never go to the officials. Too risky for everyone."

Winston nodded as he listened. He looked up at Vincent. "Now what?"

Vincent drew in a long breath and let it out slowly. "Now we turn the tables. Trip her up in her own game."

"Wouldn't it simply be easier to leave? Get away from her, start somewhere else?"

"'If Charrie is still tied to the DA in New York, there is no telling what else she may do. The thing is, Charrie has access to everything related to Tess's business. That's how much Tess trusted her. And it's all coming back to kick her in the ass." His jaw clenched. "The only way to end this once and for all is to stop it at the source.

"Look, if you would have asked me a year ago—would I risk my career, my freedom, and even my life, for a woman—especially a woman with a past like Tess?—I might have shot you." He shook his head slowly. "But Tess isn't like other women. At least no woman I've ever known." He glanced down for a moment, then back at Winston. "And I think you know that, as well," he said softly, the implication clear.

Winston lifted his chin slightly. He knew exactly how Vincent felt. There *was* no other woman like Tess McDonald, and he knew that any man who'd ever fallen under her spell was under it for good, himself included.

"We'll do it your way," Winston finally said.

"It will take a few days. . . ."

TWENTY-FOUR

TESS BOLTED UP in bed when she heard fumbling at the door. She reached for her purse, and just then Vincent walked in. Slowly she relaxed.

Vincent shut the door. "You okay?"

"Are you?"

He grimaced a bit, limped to the bed, and plopped down. He pressed his hand to his side. "Been better."

"Let me take a look." She gently lifted his shirt. "You're not bleeding."

"That's a comfort," he said, biting out the words. He lowered himself down and stretched out.

"Are you going to tell me what happened?"

Vincent threw his arm across his eyes. "I told Winston everything. He was pretty relieved to know that you weren't at the bottom of the ocean." He dropped his arm and angled his head in her direction. "You want to tell me about you and Winston?"

"He's a friend. I told you that before."

"Tess, I investigated you for months, remember? You don't just have *friends*. Not like the girl next door. So let's not bullshit each other, not now."

She ran her tongue across her lips. "Fine. What do you want to know?"

"How 'bout everything."

Tess sighed heavily, willing herself to say the words. "I was eighteen. . . ."

She took him through the months of their affair, her growing feelings for a man she knew she could never have, finally accepting that her feelings could never be reciprocated. And then he returned home. She left out the most devastating part—the child she'd carried to term and given away. Some things were best left buried.

"Thank you," he said, "for telling me."

She didn't respond. Tess got up and moved slowly to the other side of the room. "There is one more thing I should tell you."

"I'm listening."

"One of the reasons I came here was because of Winston."

Vincent went rigid. He knew the look on Winston's face when he talked about Tess—the relief when he realized that she was alive. It was love. He loved her all right, then and now.

"Don't worry, nothing has gone on between us. It's just that I knew that Winston would look out for me. He'd make sure that I was all right."

"Is that all? Did you think that maybe you could rekindle something?"

"No. I'm a realist. Winston was just starting out on his political journey when we met. He wouldn't give that up then, and I was not so delusional to believe that he'd achieved this level to give it all up now." She looked him in the eye. "Besides, even though I hated your guts, I was still in love with you."

He reached out and grabbed her hand and pulled her toward him. She tumbled down onto the bed. "Lucky for me." He stroked her face. "We're going to get all this shit straight, get away from here, and build some kind of life, me and you."

She nodded.

"There's one thing I still want to know."

"What's that?"

"Why did you ever get involved . . . in the business?"

"Humph." She laughed softly. "The age-old question. At first, it was a means to an end." She shrugged. "I guess since I was always perceived as the 'bad twin,' I began to internalize it. I wanted to be as different from my perfect, upstanding sister and as far on the opposite end of right as possible. By the time Winston came along, I was already in the game—small time, but in it.

"After he left, I went on with my life, full speed ahead. I figured if this *was* going to be my life, I had to be the best at it. I got my college degree, saved my money, shopped in the best stores, attended all the right parties, met all the right people, and I watched my business grow. No different from any other red-blooded entrepreneur."

"Except that your business is illegal."

Tess scoffed. "The only reason it's illegal is because Uncle Sam can't figure out how to tax it. Besides, my business was much more than sex for hire. The women who worked for me were educated, classy, medically scanned on a regular basis. They knew how to make any man feel like he was the most important man in the world. They could hold a conversation in any setting, hostess a party for dignitaries—and if sex was involved, it was extra and consensual—all for a very nice fee, of course."

"Of course."

"Enough about the past," she said. "I want to close the book on it. Deal?"

"On one condition."

Tess frowned. "What condition is that?"

"That tonight . . ." He flipped her onto her back. "I'm in charge."

"Did I ever mention how much I love when a man takes charge?"

"Why don't you tell me all about it . . . step by step."

THE FOLLOWING MORNING Vincent turned on his side and reached for Tess. Their night together had been off the charts, as usual. At times he was hard-pressed to separate love from lust. He knew he was completely under her spell, but was that the sex or something more?

He'd been thinking a lot lately, asking himself some tough questions. At his core, he was a law-abiding man, always had been. Growing up on the streets of Southside Chicago, he'd seen his share of violence, drugs, gangs, and all manner of illegal activity. His best friend had been gunned down right in front of him in a random drive-by shooting. That death had devastated him unlike anything else he'd ever seen. He determined from that day on to do whatever he could to put criminals behind bars, where they belonged.

According to the law, Tess was a criminal, engaged in illicit activity. And if he was the man he believed himself to be, he would see that she paid for her crimes.

Yet, he couldn't do it. He couldn't turn her in. The moral dilemma was eating away at him. Was the sex so good that he'd become blinded to what was right and what was wrong? Or had he really fallen for the fallen woman?

All he knew was that he loved Tess, like no other love he'd ever felt. Loved her enough to go against the very grain of who he was. It scared him to admit that.

He patted the side of the bed and found the space next to him empty. Squinting against the early morning sun that peeked in through the windows, he looked around the room. He sat up and rubbed the sleep from his eyes. Maybe she was in the bathroom. He called out to her and got no answer. He listened and was met with silence.

Tossing the covers off, he got up and knocked on the bathroom door. The door eased open. The room was empty. Frowning he looked around, really paying attention now. Her clothes were gone.

Maybe she went to get some air or something to eat. He got cleaned up and put on his clothes, expecting her back any minute. But as time went by, he became convinced that something was wrong.

He went out to the front desk and asked the desk clerk if he'd seen her.

"Yes," the man said brightly. "She went out about an hour ago."

Vincent hurried out to the parking lot. Her car was gone.

SHE SHOULD HAVE told Vincent she was leaving, at least left him a note. But she didn't want to risk him stopping or following her. She needed to do this her way. *Enough.* The simple word had awakened her from sleep. *Enough*. She wouldn't spend the rest of her life running. She wouldn't be party to setting someone else up again. She'd done enough harm to others, and it was time to stop.

She thought about the phone call she'd received that night from Vincent, not so long ago: *You can't continue to get away with ruining people's lives, Tess. I won't let you. Not this time.* He was right. She couldn't keep living the way she was. At the center of everything that had happened in the past year, she was there pulling the strings, like a master puppeteer. And whether Vincent realized it or not, he *had* stopped her. He'd made her realize what was really important in this life. His willingness to give up everything for her finally showed her that she was valued, something she'd been searching for all her life. And if she was going to have any kind of life and be deserving of that man, then *enough*.

She slowed the car just outside the villa. Everything seemed quiet. It was still early, just past daybreak. She parked and walked the rest of the way, steeling her resolve with every step.

Reaching the front door, she used her key and let herself in. Nothing moved. She went down the hallway and up the stairs to the bedrooms above. Charrie's room was at the end of the hall.

She stood in front of the door, hesitating for a moment. Silently she turned the knob and stepped inside, shutting the door behind her. Charrie stirred, but she didn't wake up.

For a moment Tess just watched her, remembering the young girl she'd met ten years earlier, whom she'd entrusted with every aspect of her life. What had she done to make Charrie turn against her and make Tess her enemy?

Tess approached the bed and stood over Charrie. Sensing a presence, Charrie opened her eyes. It took a moment to focus, and when she did, she scrambled to the other side of the bed in disbelief and fear.

"No. I'm not a ghost come to haunt you," Tess said with cool calm.

"But . . ."

Tess offered a sad smile. "I know, you wanted me dead and you convinced Kim and Nicole to do it. I want to know why."

Charrie's expression quickly shifted from fear to abhorrence. "Why?" She jumped up out of the bed, keeping it between them. "Because you needed to pay for what you'd done to me."

Tess's face twisted in confusion. "What I'd done to you? What did I do to you besides look after you, give you a life and every comfort you could imagine."

Charrie tossed her head back and laughed. "Even now, you're still a sanctimonious bitch! What you've done for me . . . I'll tell you what you've done: you didn't even bother to give me a name." Tears of rage filled her eyes but didn't fall. "You didn't care enough to keep me. You gave me away like used clothes so that you could live your life as a high-priced whore! Fucking men for a living was more important to you than your own child!" There, she'd said it.

Tess felt her knees wobble. *No.* Her stomach clenched. She shook her head back and forth in disbelief. "That's not possible."

"Isn't it?" she screamed. She tore across the room and flung open her closet. She took out the old lockbox.

Tess saw it and remembered. Her heart raced. *It can't be.* She could barely breathe.

Charrie opened the box and pulled out the documents that had changed her life. She flung them at Tess. They fell at her feet.

"Read them, and then you tell me it's not possible." Charrie's chest heaved in and out with exertion. She gripped the edge of the dresser as she glared at Tess.

Trancelike, Tess leaned down and picked up the papers. Her hand shook. She kept telling herself as she unfolded them that she would find some glitch, some mistake to make this all go away. But as she read and she remembered and saw the evidence of her damning signature. . . .

She looked up at Charrie, who hadn't moved from the spot by the dresser. "I . . . didn't know it was you."

Charrie didn't respond.

"Charrie you've got to believe me I—"

"Did you even have a name for me?"

"I was nineteen years old," she said, pleading for understanding.

"Single mothers do it every day. But I guess that doesn't apply to single whores!"

Tess flinched. "You don't understand—"

"No. I don't think I ever will."

"I made the only choice that made sense to me then. I wanted you to have a life, not the kind of life that I was living."

"But I lived it anyway." She sputtered a sad laugh. "How ironic is that?"

"Charrie . . ." She faltered, not knowing what to say and knowing that mere words would never make it right. "Why didn't you tell me when you found out?"

Charrie snapped her head away. "I was so . . . so hurt." She turned to Tess, her stare burning into her. She balled her hands into tight fists. "I felt betrayed, used. I looked at you and all that you had become, the life you chose instead of choosing me, and all I could think about was hurting you as badly as I was hurt."

"I am so terribly sorry. Giving you up was the hardest thing I ever had to do. You have to believe that."

Charrie wiped her eyes. "I thought that hurting the one thing you cherished would fill this hole in my heart." She pressed her fist to chest. "But it's still empty." She slid down the wall and sobbed, burying her face against her knees.

Tess ran over and crouched down next to her. She pulled her into her arms. "Charrie, I can't undo the past. I can't make what you've gone through go away. But I can start from here to be as much of a mother to you as you'll let me."

She made a weak effort to pull away.

"I know how desperate you must have become to strike back. I know about desperation and thinking that hurting someone else will make life livable again. It never does. Living your life for revenge will eat you alive. You can spend the rest of your life hating me. I wouldn't blame you. But a life filled with hate is not a life at all."

Slowly Tess got up. "I'm staying at the Cove . . . with Vincent. I'll be there a couple more days, and then I'm leaving, giving up the business. You can have the business and everything that goes with it. It's what you wanted." She moved to the door.

Charrie's head snapped up. "Wait!"

Tess looked at her.

"Do you . . . even know who my father is?"

Her father had no idea that he had a child. Now more than ever he could be ruined by a scandal, a child conceived during his marriage. But it was the one thing in his life that he felt he'd lost out on. He deserved to know, and it was time that Charrie knew her father, as well.

"Yes. I know." She looked across at her. "I was in love with him."

The stiffness in Charrie's body dissolved. Her shoulders slumped. She stared at Tess as if the words didn't make sense.

"He wasn't in love with me, and he was married at the time." She lowered her eyes in shame.

That revelation was the last one she'd expected. From the moment she'd discovered that Tess was her mother and the kind of life she'd lived, she was committed to believing that Tess had no knowledge of the identity of her father. Now the hatred she'd held on to became sorrow, and tears spilled down her cheeks.

A part of her still needed to hold on to that last kernel of pain; otherwise, all that she'd done—the compromises she'd made, the lives she jeopardized—would have been for nothing.

"Get out. Go," she ground out, unable to look at Tess.

Tess hesitated, took a step toward Charrie, then retreated.

"I'll be at the Cove if you want to see me." She opened the door and walked out.

Her legs felt like lead as she went down the staircase. She gripped the railing to keep from falling. Her heart ached so deeply, she was sure it would break. Charrie . . . her daughter.

God, had she known all these years and simply pretended it wasn't true? Had she seen herself in her daughter but refused to accept it?

From the beginning, there was some connection between them and her gut made her think that maybe, just maybe it was possible. Mother's intuition? A trait she didn't believe she possessed. Was that why she never allowed her protégée to "date" the clients, out of maternal instinct?

A dizzying array of thoughts and emotions swirled through her at once, leaving her worn out. Blindly she got to her car. It took her several attempts before she was able to get the key in the lock.

She heard someone behind her. They were calling her name.

She barely glanced back. It was Kim.

She couldn't face her now. She had nothing left. She got in her car and drove away just as Kim ran to the car door.

TWENTY-FIVE

CHARRIE PICKED HERSELF UP from the floor and dragged herself to her bed. All this time, the months of rage and anger were meaningless. Her obsession with ruining Tess had consumed her, and now with no more fuel for her fire, she didn't know what to do with her emotions or where to turn.

She didn't know who she was anymore. For years, she'd believed she was the daughter of Mr. and Mrs. Lewis only to discover that in truth she was the daughter of a prostitute. She'd latched on to that knowledge and the notion that she was fathered by some unknown trick. The images had distorted her thinking, her view of herself. She'd become someone without roots, without a soul. She fed on that belief to the exclusion of everything. Her focus become retribution, pain, hurt, and suffering.

Yet, at the moment when she could have rid herself of that

albatross, she didn't. She shot Vincent instead. Ever since that night, she'd questioned her actions and the answer was always the same: Tess was her mother, and as much as she'd hated her for what she'd done, she also loved her.

That knowledge tore at her from the inside out, shifting between love and hate and back again.

She hadn't been conceived in some back alley or some ratty hotel bed. Her mother had loved her father. *God!*

She pulled at her hair, spun around in the room, and screamed and screamed until her throat was raw.

Nicole came running to her door, burst in, and saw Charrie crumpled on the floor. Kim rushed in behind her.

"Tess was here," she whispered to Nicole, grabbing her by the arm.

Nicole stared wide-eyed at Kim.

Charrie raised her head. Her face was a portrait of anguish. "My mother," she mumbled.

"What?" Nicole said, thinking that Charrie had truly lost it if she was asking for her mother.

"She's . . . my mother . . . I tried to have you kill my mother. I'm so sorry, Mama," she sobbed. "I'm so sorry." She covered her face with her hands and wept.

VINCENT FLUNG OPEN THE DOOR, ready to go looking for Tess and found her standing on the other side.

"Tess. What the hell—?"

She walked past him as if he wasn't there. Like a robot she sat down in the chair by the window, staring out at the lush landscape beyond.

Vincent shut the door. "Tess." He came to her side, knelt down in front of her. His eyes raced up and down her body. "Are you all right? Are you hurt?"

She didn't respond.

"Hey." He shook her by the shoulders. "Talk to me. What is it?"

Her eyes were vacant when she looked at him. "She's my daughter," she said in a monotone.

"Who? What are you talking about?"

"Charrie."

"You're not making any sense."

"Charrie is my daughter." She turned her head and stared out the window again.

Vincent rocked back on his haunches. He shook his head. It didn't make sense. Tess didn't have kids. She would have told him. Wouldn't she?

"Please, you need to tell me what's going on. What happened? Where did you go?"

She sighed heavily, then pressed her fist to her mouth to keep from screaming.

"Baby, talk to me, please."

Her eyes rose to meet the concern in his. Her bottom lip trembled.

"Please. Whatever it is, just talk to me."

Between silent tears, bit by bit she told him about the child she'd given birth to at the age of nineteen and given away without so much as ever seeing it or knowing its sex. She told him about Charrie's discovery among her adoptive parents' papers and her ensuing quest to ruin her mother. Finally she told him about Winston—the father of her child.

Silence entered the room and sat between them. Shaken, Vin-

cent finally pushed to his feet. He shoved his hands into his pockets. He didn't know what to do with what he'd heard, how to deal
with it. It wasn't so much that Tess had a child but all the other
circumstances surrounding it. He couldn't imagine the level of
anguish Charrie must have felt to work so hard to get back at
Tess—from turning informant to wanting her killed. What tor-
ture that must have been.

"What are you going to do now?" he asked as gently as he could.

She shook her head. "I don't know."

"This could have gone so wrong." He let out a breath. "You
gave her an opening. It's up to her now if she decides to take it."
Then he asked the question that he dreaded asking but knew that
he must. "What about Winston? Do you plan to tell him?"

"I hadn't thought that far," she said, sounding like a lost child.

"Best that it comes from you sooner rather than later. He de-
serves to know."

She looked up at him. "Do you hate me now?"

"Tess . . . how could I hate you? What I hate is what all this, the
secrets, the past has done to everyone. What it's done to you. We
all make mistakes. You did what you thought was best. And she
had a good life with her adoptive parents—she's said as much to
you herself."

"Yes, she did." She nodded her head and sniffed. "I'm thankful
for that."

"But why would you keep something like that from me?"

"I never thought . . ."

"Is there anything else I should know?" he asked, tensing.

She looked at his hard stance, the set of his shoulders. Vincent
may love her, he may have given up his career for her, he may have
accepted her past life and even forgiven her for it, but he would

never, ever understand what she'd done that night back in New York. Never.

"No. There's nothing else."

He said, "When you're ready, I'm going with you to tell Winston," and took her into his arms. "You're not alone anymore, Tess."

TWENTY-SIX

AVERY SAT in his high-back black leather chair behind the gleaming wood desk. All along the paneled walls were plaques witnessing his successes in law enforcement over the years. He'd risen up the ranks from a law student clerking for the judge to getting his JD, landing a job in the prosecutors office all the way up to district attorney. He'd vowed to do right by the people of New York, see justice done and people treated fairly. But politics and justice were strange bedfellows.

Over time he'd gone from a naïve hot shot pledging liberty and justice for all to a man who'd compromised his values for money, fame, and the most wicked evil of all—power. He'd used his friends and anyone else who would serve his purposes. Now all his manipulations had come home to roost. His reelection bid was only weeks away, and his opponent was winning in all the polls.

He'd been so sure that if he could finally prosecute the elusive Madame X, he would slide into victory and somehow tie her to two murders. He'd given Vincent all the ammunition he needed, he'd put him on the scent, but his agent had turned. He'd banked on Tracy's zeal to put it all together, a case that none of his other prosecutors could handle, but time was running out.

The wall-mounted television projected a picture but no sound. He didn't want to hear what the pundits had to say about his chances of reelection. His opponent, a Democrat, was ahead by twenty-five percentage points. He pointed the remote at the television and shut it off.

He had to do something, turn the last screw. He refused to go down without a fight.

Avery reached for the phone and dialed Tracy in Colorado. She owed him, and she was overdue.

TRACY STARED at the caller ID on her phone. She knew who it was, and was in no mood or frame of mind to speak with Avery. She knew what he wanted. She went to the closet in the foyer and got her coat. The hospital had called. They'd moved Mark out of ICU and into a private room.

When she arrived at the hospital, several of Mark's buddies were just leaving.

"He looks like crap, but his spirits are good," one of the guys said as she approached.

"Thanks." During the initial days of his recovery, she'd spent so much time around the men from his engine company, she was like one of the guys. It was an odd kind of camaraderie, and touched her deeply. But there was an unwritten rule among firefighters that if any of them were hurt or killed in the line of duty, they would take it upon themselves to make sure that the injured or lost fire-fighter's wife, girlfriend, or family was looked after.

It was an entirely new experience for her. She'd never had many girlfriends, and in her line of work it was so cutthroat, you didn't dare make too many friends. Besides, the burnout from the workload alone canceled out many friendships before they got started. Prosecutors came and went as though through a revolving door. There was no point in becoming attached.

"My wife is making potluck this weekend. You're welcome to stop by and hang out if you want," Mark's friend Andrew said.

"I'll definitely keep that in mind. Thanks for asking."

"Sure." He bobbed his head and walked away.

Tracy peeked in the room. Mark looked asleep. She tiptoed inside and eased her coat and bag into the chair next to the bed.

"Even with slits for eyes, I'd know you anywhere," came the very hoarse voice.

Tracy grinned and went over to the bed. She leaned against the railing and looked down and him. "Damn, you look like you've been in a fight."

"You should see the other guy."

They'd taken him out from under the plastic covering. The oxygen was coursing through the short plastic tubes in his nose. The bruising was easing up, and she knew in another couple of weeks he would look like the Mark she knew.

"How are you feeling?"

"Like I fell through a roof." He tried to laugh and started coughing. Gradually the hacks subsided.

"You have to take it easy," she warned, stroking his brow.

"Yeah, the doctors said I can leave in about a week."

"Really?" Her eyes widened in surprise. "That's wonderful."

"The bad news is, I really shouldn't be alone."

"You're going to stay with me. That was never an issue."

"Are you sure?"

"Absolutely. It never occurred to me that you would go home to an empty apartment." She stepped closer. "We're a couple, re-member, a team. We'll do this together."

"I can be a real grumpy pain in the ass."

"Then I'll just ignore you." She grinned. "It'll be fine. Besides, it will give me a chance to test the waters."

"Waters?" His mouth quirked into a smile.

"Yes, future waters. I need to see if I can still swim." She leaned closer and playfully ran her finger across his chest. "I have it all planned. We'll camp out downstairs so you don't have to go up and down until your leg is stronger. And I still work at the library a few days a week, so I can get out of your hair and you can get out of mine, and—"

He reached for her with his bandaged hand, cutting her off. "I'm a great swimmer . . . and I promise I won't let you go under."

Her eyes searched his and found sincerity—and devotion. It had been so long since she'd given herself permission to care about anyone or anything other than her job and getting ahead. It was all new, but she was determined to make herself ready and damn the rest. Maybe if she tried especially hard, she really could become Victoria Styles. But to do that, she would have to sever her ties with her past once and for all.

TWENTY-SEVEN

"SHE REALLY HAS LOST HER MIND," Nicole said, stealing a glance over her shoulder as they hurried down the hallway. "Tess? Her mother? Come on. The bitch is crazy, plain and simple."

Kim had seen Tess's face the moment before she tore away in the car. That wasn't the face of someone who'd been confronted by someone crazy. That was the face of a woman who'd confronted a hard truth.

"So now what?" Nicole asked. "She knows Tess ain't dead. There's no telling what she will get in her head to do to us."

"What if she's telling the truth?"

"Say what? No way. You mean to tell me Tess was tricking out her own daughter?"

"I don't know what kind of arrangement they had, but what if Charrie is telling the truth and Tess is her mother?"

"Umph, that would be some shit." She shook her head. "I don't believe it, though. We've thought a lot of things about Tess, but that would be really ugly."

"Maybe Tess didn't know."

"You're in la–la land."

"Maybe I am, but what if I'm not?" She walked off, leaving Nicole standing in the hallway.

Nicole stood there for a few moments. If Charrie was as crazy as she thought, there was no way that Tess would allow her to continue to run the business. Tess wanted out, she'd said as much up on the cliff. And she was getting a feeling that Kim wasn't so keen on the whole idea of running an escort service as she once was. That left her. She smiled. Maybe all this crazy shit would work out after all.

KIM SAT on the side of her bed and took her cell phone from the nightstand. She searched for Tess's phone number and dialed.

Tess felt the vibration of her phone through her purse. She pulled it out, saw the number. She hesitated for a moment. She didn't have the energy to deal with Kim right now, but she also knew she couldn't put it off indefinitely. She stole a glance at Vincent, who had his eyes on the road.

"Yes?"

"I want to know what's going on, Tess. I have a right to know. What is Charrie talking about? She was rambling on about you being her mother, for God's sake."

Tess swallowed. "It's true."

Kim clenched the phone. "What?"

"It's true. Charrie is my daughter."

The car jerked when Vincent suddenly hit the brake. He snapped his head in her direction. She held up her hand to let him know it was all right. *It's okay,* she mouthed.

"I'll explain everything, but right now I have something I need to take care of."

"Look, I don't understand any of this. It's not what I signed on for. You made promises," she added, biting out each word. She saw all that she'd done, all that she'd given up, flash before her eyes.

"I know, and I intend to keep them. All I ask is that you be a little patient."

"Patient! Everything is coming apart. I should never have listened to you in the beginning. I should never have bought into that—that fantasy of yours that we could get rid of our problems and simply walk away. Trouble has followed us every step of the way, and the only one in this mess with clean hands is you!"

Tess wanted to tell her that she'd always had free will—the will to do what she wanted—and she'd wanted her husband dead. She'd bought into the fantasy for all her own reasons. Tess hadn't twisted her arm. She hadn't twisted Nicole's either. Revenge drove them to do what they did. She didn't push Trust over that balcony. She didn't rig Troy's car. She'd tapped into their dark sides, the side that no one ever talks about—the "what if" corner of their souls.

But the honest truth was, she was as guilty as they were. She'd seen into the darkness, read their needs, and fed their desires. Her hands would never be clean.

"You still have a choice. You can choose to be patient like I asked, or not. It's up to you."

Winston's estate was coming into view. "I have to go. I'll call you later, and we'll work things out. That I promise." She disconnected the call before Kim could protest, then powered off her phone.

KIM STARED at the phone for a moment. She got up from the side of the bed, grabbed a jacket from the back of the door, and went out. She needed to get away. She couldn't think. She ran downstairs and out the door, got in one of the cars, and drove off.

"WHO WAS THAT?" Vincent asked as he pulled up to the gate.

"It was Kim."

He stared at her. "She want to set up another meeting—push you out into traffic this time?"

"Charrie told her about me. She wanted to know what was going on. That's all."

The intercom chirped.

"Vincent and Tess. Winston is expecting us."

The gate creaked open.

Earl met them at the door.

Vincent could only imagine the stories that guy could tell, he mused as they followed the butler down the hall to the study.

Winston was on the phone when they got to the door. He looked up and waved them in. Earl backed away as quietly as he had arrived.

Tess and Vincent took seats in two matching armchairs. Winston concluded his call.

He came around the desk, went over to Tess, and took her hand. "Thank God you're all right." He squeezed it tightly, and

Vincent knew that had he not been there, Winston's greeting would have been much more than a little hand-holding.

"There are some things I need to tell you." She looked at Vincent.

"I'll leave you two alone." He got up and walked out.

Winston's face creased in concern. "What is it?"

"Remember when we met," she began.

He smiled gently. "Of course I do. Why?"

She drew in a breath and looked directly at him. "After you left to come back to Aruba . . ."

Tess told him everything—from her pregnancy to meeting Charrie years later, taking her into the business, up to and including all that she'd found out Charrie had done and her reasons why.

Nearly an hour later, she sat tensely waiting for Winston's response. She'd watched his expressions vacillate between shock, disappointment, and disbelief to acceptance and back again.

When she was finished, it was dead silent. Winston got up from sitting next to her and walked to the other side of the room

He kept his back to her. "I loved you, you know."

Her heart jumped.

He turned to look at her. "If there had been any way I could have stayed, I would have." He shook his head sadly. "But I couldn't. I've regretted it every day of my life, even more so now. Had I stayed, none of this would be happening."

She got up. "You can't blame yourself, Winston. We both made choices."

"Selfish choices."

She lowered her head.

"Does she know about me?"

"No. She didn't ask. All she wanted to know was if I even knew who her father was." She watched him flinch at the implication.

"I see." He heaved a sigh. "Now what?"

"She needs to know you. You both deserve that much. But I don't know how it will affect your standing here."

"To hell with my standing! My worrying about what people would think is why we're here today, talking about a daughter that neither of us knew about for twenty-five years."

How different would her life have been if Winston had divorced his wife and stayed with her to raise their child? She would never have continued in the "profession." She would never have gotten caught up in the wicked game of murder. Troy would still be alive, and so would Trust—for what it was worth—and Kim and Nicole would have had to find their own way to deal with the men in their lives. Their paths and their futures would have never crossed and become forever entwined. One act, one decision had set them all on a course they could never have imagined.

"Where is she now?" Winston asked.

"At the villa."

"We need to go and see her. Both of us."

She nodded in agreement and relief.

Vincent was sitting in the lounge area, sipping a cup of tea, which he hated. He hadn't wanted to seem rude when Earl brought it out on a silver tray.

"We're going back to the villa . . . to talk to Charrie," Tess said as she and Winston approached.

Vincent glanced from one face to the other, trying to read something, anything, in their eyes. Tess walked over to him, seeming to sense his uncertainty, and kissed him lightly on the mouth. "Everything is going to be okay," she said softly.

He put his hand on her waist. "I'm going to hold you to that," he said, for her ears only.

"I think I should drive over with Winston."

"I'll wait for you at the hotel."

"Thank you."

He watched them walk out. *The things a man does for a woman,* he mused, *and that woman in particular.*

THEY DIDN'T TALK MUCH on the drive over, each of them captured by their own swirling thoughts, coming to terms with all that had transpired.

"I think I should talk to her first, prepare her," Tess finally said as they approached the villa.

"Whatever you think is best." He thought of all the times he'd seen Charrie and been charmed by her grace and her beauty—so much like her mother, he realized with a jolt. She always reminded him of Tess on the few occasions when he saw her, but he'd attributed that impression to them having been so close for so long and unconsciously assuming many of the same qualities.

They pulled up in front of the house, parked in the driveway, and got out.

Tess looked up at the house and the surrounding grounds. She'd had big dreams coming here. She was going to start over, with new faces, a new approach, and leave the past behind her. She was going to provide a new life for Kim and Nicole in payment for what they'd done at her behest. None of it had worked. And maybe it wasn't supposed to. Maybe they were supposed to come here, but not to start over, but to face the things they could never run far enough away from. She didn't know anymore.

"I'll go and find her," Tess said when they stepped inside. "Why don't you wait down here?"

"Are you sure?"

"I'll be fine."

She headed for the stairs. The house was quiet. Unless they were entertaining, the only people on the grounds were Charrie, Nicole, and Kim. At least she wouldn't have to run the gauntlet of guests. She reached the top of the stairs just as Nicole came out of her room.

"What's going on?" she asked.

"I came back to talk to Charrie. Where's Kim?"

"I heard a car pull off a little while ago. I guess she went out." She stared at Tess. "Is it true about you being Charrie's mother?"

"Yes."

Nicole looked away. "Damn. I thought I'd seen my share of dysfunctional families, but this tops it all."

"It's not what you think."

"So what is it, then?"

"I can't talk to you about this now. But I will." She left her standing there and went to Charrie's room.

The door was slightly ajar. Tess pushed it open. Charrie was on the bed, facedown. Her room was turned upside down, as if a child had a major temper tantrum.

Tess stepped inside and shut the door behind her.

Charrie stirred and turned onto her back. Her nostrils flared. "What are you doing here?"

"I didn't want to wait until you came to me." She approached slowly. "You asked me if I knew your father, and I told you I did, but you never asked who he is."

"What does it matter?" she said, the sadness in her voice so heavy, it weighed her down.

"It matters because he wants to meet you."

"What?" She sat up, staring at Tess with mistrust.

"He's here, and he wants to meet you."

TWENTY-EIGHT

KIM WASN'T SURE where she was going, why, or what she hoped to accomplish once she arrived. All she did know was that she needed to get away from the place that now represented everything that had gone so very wrong in her life.

What was she going to do? She'd given up everything. Her company, what was left of it, was no more than a shell. She'd seen visions of financial freedom and a new lease on life by coming here. She'd needed a way out, and once again Tess had provided it for her. And once again, it had gone terribly wrong.

She drove along the busy streets of downtown, found a parking space, and got out. The walkways were teeming with tourists and vendors. The swell of appetizing aromas drifting out from the rows of outdoor cafés settled right in her stomach. She was starving.

She walked along the street, trying to decide where she wanted to stop, when she heard someone calling out to her. She looked past the heads of passersby and spotted a waving hand.

It was Clarke. Her heart felt like it stumbled in her chest.

He darted around the strolling tourists until he was in front of her, a big smile stretching his mouth. "I thought that was you," he said, a bit breathless. "I noticed you when you got out of the car."

"Oh. Good to see you." She started to move away; he gently clasped her upper arm.

"Wait. Are you shopping, meeting someone?"

"I was looking for someplace to have lunch, actually."

"Alone?"

"Yes. Why?"

"I'm starving, myself. If you don't mind, we can have lunch together." When she didn't answer, he went on. "I did say I wanted to talk to you some more about your ideas. This seems to be fate."

"I . . . sure, why not. Do you have someplace in mind?"

"Not really. And I'm easy to please."

She flashed him a look.

"Meaning, food. I love just about everything." He held up a finger. "Except anchovies." He shook his head vigorously and screwed up his face.

Kim had to laugh. "I'll keep that in mind."

Clarke jerked his head toward a small café on the opposite side of the street. "I've been there. Food is great and the service is wonderful."

"Fine."

They crossed the street, and Kim was surprised to feel Clarke's hand at the small of her back. She wasn't sure if he was merely being a gentleman guiding her across the street or if he thought he had the right to touch her.

A young woman with beautiful dimples greeted them at the door of the restaurant. "Welcome to Adam and Eve. How many for lunch?"

"Two," Clarke said.

"Would you prefer garden seating or something inside?"

"Garden," they both said at once, then turned to each other and laughed.

They were shown to seats that looked out at the ocean.

"Great choice," Kim said.

"Glad you like it. Wait until you taste the food."

She scanned the menu. "How much longer will you be staying?" she asked.

"That's what I wanted to talk to you about."

She put down her menu and looked over at him. "Me?"

His expression went from amicable to staid. "I know who you really are."

TWENTY-NINE

"I DON'T BELIEVE YOU. How could my father be here?"

"He's been here all along. Since he left the States."

Charrie got up from the bed. "It's another one of your lies." Her chest heaved in and out.

"It's the truth, Charrie. What reason would I have to lie to you about something like that—after everything that's happened? He wants to meet you."

Charrie spun away. Her thoughts raced. Her father? Had she walked right past him all these months, not knowing? Had he been here to the villa? He must know what she does for a living. Will he look at her with disgust or love? "Will you be there with me?" she asked softly, suddenly afraid.

"Yes. Of course."

She nodded slowly. "Could you . . . give me a minute please? I'll come down."

"Sure." Tess walked out and went down to join Winston.

He jumped up from his seat the moment he saw her coming down the stairs. He looked past her for Charrie.

"Where is she? What happened?"

She pressed her hand to his shoulder. "She's coming."

He exhaled a long breath of relief. "I don't even know what to say to her," he confessed.

"Tell her the truth."

"I—"

Charrie was coming down the stairs. Winston seemed to truly see her for the very first time. And at that moment she was no longer the sleek, sophisticated beauty; she was an uncertain, disillusioned, and scared young girl.

She stopped at the bottom of the stairs, looked at Tess and then Winston, her expression was one of confusion. "I thought you said—"

Tess took Winston's hand. "Charrie, Winston is your father."

Charrie swayed for a moment, and Winston reached out to grab her. He ushered her over to the couch. His arm was around her shoulders. "I know," he said gently, "I felt the same way."

She looked into his green eyes. "You?"

"Me."

"All this time . . . I've been to your house, I . . . told you those lies . . . Oh God!" She covered her face.

Winston pulled her hands away and held them down on her lap. Tears rolled down her cheeks.

"Listen to me. A great deal of things have happened over the years. We all made mistakes. We all did things we regret. No one is without fault here. But the truth is out now. And if we can be anything to each other, we're going to need to start now and start forgiving."

"I don't know where to begin," Charrie wept.

"Well, why don't I start by telling you about me. . . ."

Tess eased off to the side to give them some space. It was remarkable to watch Winston with her. He got her to smile, and he touched her tenderly as they spoke. It was so natural to him—as if he'd taken care of her all his life. She could see Charrie's tension begin to soften as she nodded and responded to whatever Winston was saying.

It would be so much easier for Charrie to open her heart to Winston, to forgive him for not being around. It was not his fault that he didn't step into the role of father and wasn't there for her. She'd deprived Winston of the choice, and they'd all paid dearly for her decision.

They didn't notice her leave. She went out back to the pool. She sat on the edge, took off her shoes, and put her feet in the water. An innocent act, something so simple, sitting by the pool, wading bare feet in the water. If only her life were this simple and innocent.

Tess looked at the beauty surrounding her. She'd brought nothing but ugliness here. It wasn't often that she had attacks of conscience. She'd lived her life doing exactly what she wanted, getting hers whenever she wanted. She'd manipulated peoples' lives for as far back as she could remember. It was her skill, the one thing she was truly good at. But at what cost?

"I saw Charrie inside with Winston."

Tess looked up, shielded her eyes from the sun with her palm. Nikki was standing over her. She turned her face away.

"Is he—?"

"Yes, that's her father."

"Damn. The prime minister. Did he know?"

Tess shook her head.

Nicole lowered herself down next to Tess. "What now?"

"I don't know."

"Are you still planning on leaving?"

"Yes." She looked at Nicole. "What about you?"

"I've been thinking that I would stay."

"Why?"

"There's nothing for me back in the States. I figure if I stay here, I could run things with Charrie." It was more of a question than a statement.

"I don't know what Charrie plans to do after all this. It would be her decision." She paused a moment. "I'm sorry, Nicole, for everything, for dragging you and Kim into all this."

"We knew what we were getting into from the beginning. We could have walked away, but we didn't. Everyone got what they deserved," she said with conviction. "Do I regret it? No, not one minute out of any day."

"What about Kim?"

"Kim is a big girl. She'll handle her business and make her own decision."

"What about your family? Do you plan to look for them?"

The bravado evaporated from her demeanor. "I think about Ricky and Julia every day, you know," she said wistfully. "I think about that day I came home and everything was gone. I think about sleeping on the damp wood floor thinking that when I woke up they would come back and tell me it was all a big mistake. But they didn't come back. They left me without even so much as a kiss-my-ass note." She laughed sadly. "What if I found them, Tess? What if I found them and Ricky shut the door on me? I don't think I could take it. I don't." She sniffed and averted her head. "So rather than deal with that kind of rejection again, I'll make a life for myself without them."

"The only advice I can offer you is not to make the same mistakes I did—by not giving them the chance to make the decision. If you do, you'll always be haunted by the question of what if. The villa is paid for for the next six months. Your choice." She pushed herself up just as Charrie and Winston stepped out onto the pool deck. Tess's heart pounded in her chest. She walked over to them.

Nicole slipped away.

"I'm going to go to the house," Winston said. "I need to prepare my staff about my daughter." He looked at Charrie and smiled. "There's going to be plenty of speculation and accusations, but I'm ready for them."

"Winston, there're going to be questions about her mother. There are people here that know . . . about me."

"I'll deal with it."

Tess vigorously shook her head. "No. I can't let you do that."

"I'm up for re-election in six months. I can ride it out. Besides, maybe it's time for me to retire anyway and start enjoying life for a change."

Tess stared at him in wonder. "You can't mean that. Politics has been everything to you. You worked so hard to get where you are."

"Yes, and I let my career, my family, and everyone else's expectations drive me. It's time for *me* now."

"Are you sure?"

"Never more sure of anything."

"You don't have to do this," Charrie said. "We can . . . find a way to work things out between us without damaging you. No one has to know."

"Yes, they do," he said with all sincerity. "You deserve to be recognized. I'm not going to keep you in the shadows now that I've found you. The only thing I've ever wanted more than a stellar career has been a child of my own. I didn't have that with my wife. And now that we've found each other, I'm not going to waste another minute."

Charrie's eyes filled with tears. She didn't know what to say.

"So," he drew in a breath. "I better get home. Call me later, and we'll talk some more, make some plans." He leaned down and kissed the top of her head, then walked away.

Charrie and Tess faced each other, not as partners but as mother and daughter. Finally.

"I'm making arrangements to stay at one of the hotels downtown." Charrie looked behind her. "I can't stay here any longer."

Tess nodded. "I understand."

Charrie looked at her mother, opened her mouth as if she was going to speak, but suddenly turned and ran into the house, leaving Tess with nothing but her conscience to keep her company.

THIRTY

KIM'S CHEEKS FLAMED RED. "I'm sure I don't know what you mean."
She sputtered a nervous laugh and reached for her glass of water.

"You're quite a brilliant woman—of course you know what I
mean. You're Kimberly Shepherd-Benning, former CEO of Shepherd Enterprises, one of the most diverse corporations on Wall
Street."

She couldn't breathe. The last thing she'd expected was for
someone to realize who she was. It was one of the reasons that
the women who came to the villa used only first names.

"I didn't tell you that to make you uncomfortable or blow the
whistle on you and your friends, if that's what you're thinking."

She dared to look at him.

"When we met a few nights ago, I was utterly fascinated by
you. Not by the person you 'represented,' but by the person that

came across when you started to talk. Listening to you, your views, and ideas, I knew that you were much more than a 'hostess.' "

"What do you want? You must want something, or else you wouldn't have bothered with your revelation," she tossed back, regaining her footing.

"See, that's what I admire. Your take-no-prisoners attitude. It's just the kind of attitude and vision," he added "that I need on my team."

She frowned. "What team?"

"I'm forming a new company. I've done all that I can do and gone as far as I can where I am now. It's time for me to strike out on my own. I have the financing to get started, and what I need is a partner who can see beyond paperwork."

She couldn't be understanding him correctly. "You're asking me to be a partner in your business?"

"Exactly."

"Let's stop playing games. What do you really want?"

"I'm not playing. I assure you." He reached down by his side and picked up a thin leather portfolio and placed it on the table between them. He flipped it open, then turned it around for Kim to read. "The plan, the agreements, the projections—everything is in there. Please, just look at it."

Kim stared at him for a moment. She lowered her gaze and began to read. The more she read, the more excited she grew. But she kept her poker face, something she'd learned long ago in the boardroom with the big boys.

She was so engrossed, she didn't notice that the waitress had come and Clarke had ordered for them both. The arrival of their food made her look up.

"I hope you like steamed fish and dumplings," he said.

"Uh, yes, I do. Thank you." She kept reading through to the last page before touching her food.

Clarke waited, hoping she'd say something.

Kim glanced up from her food, reached for her glass of water, and took a long swallow. She put down the glass. "How did you know who I was?"

"After we left the villa, I went back to my hotel. I couldn't get your face and our conversation out of my head. You seemed vaguely familiar, but I couldn't place you. The only thing I was damned certain of was that you were much more than a stunning hostess. You knew business, inside and out, and that came from someone who'd lived it. So, I did what most people do when they are trying to find something: I used the Internet. I did a search on women named Kim who'd owned or run major corporations in the U.S. There were quite a few, actually, but I slowly narrowed it down and found an article in *Fortune* magazine—your picture was next to the article."

She felt her stomach sink. "I think I'd better go." She made a move to get up. Clarke grabbed her wrist.

"Please. Don't. Please, just sit down and hear me out." His eyes implored her.

Reluctantly she sat back down.

Clarke leaned across the table. His stare bore into her. "I don't know how or why you got here. I don't want to know. What I do know is that this isn't you. This isn't your life or what you were cut out for. I can offer you something more."

"You don't know anything about me."

"I know enough. I know what counts. Once I realized who you really were, I dug up your background, how you'd built your business from scratch and continued to expand for more than a decade. If you can look me in the eye and say that this life here in Aruba is what you truly want, I swear on the Queen's crown that I'll walk away and forget this conversation and our meeting ever happened."

Kim wavered. She wanted to believe him. Maybe she needed to believe him. But what if this was a ruse to make her confess to something? What would she do if this were a potential new endeavor for her corporation?

She folded her hands in front of her. "I think your proposal sounds very interesting. But I never make split-second business decisions. Before I answer you one way or the other, I'll need to review a few things first. If you can give me a day or so, I'll get back to you with my decision."

A slow smile slid across Clarke's mouth. "That is precisely why I want you at my side." He raised his glass to her. "I'll await your decision."

He dug into his food and talked about his life in London, his goals, his childhood, and family. Kim watched and listened, becoming more fascinated with him by the minute. He was incredibly handsome, intelligent, funny, and he had inexplicably fired up her sexuality. That's something she would have to keep in check. She didn't need her growing desire for him to influence her decision.

Before they knew it, the meal was over and they were back on the street.

"Thank you for lunch," she said.

"No, thank you. It was my pleasure. I hope that you will consider many more lunches."

The corner of her mouth curved. "I'll call you."

He nodded as she turned and headed back to her car.

On the drive back to the villa, she went over and over every minute of their conversation, from the initial meeting to their parting. She knew by the time she'd reached the third page of his prospectus that he had a sure winner on his hands. Land and building development that the average citizen would love—communities that incorporated the feel of each neighborhood providing schools, shopping, commercial spaces, and true affordable housing in enclosed grounds. The targeted communities would be automatically guaranteed housing while they were temporarily displaced during construction. In addition, the first jobs during the development would go straight to the residents of the communities. It was a win–win situation for everyone involved. Already her mind was reeling with ideas.

But the thought that struck her most was that if Clarke had put together who she was, someone else could do the same. And the next person might not be as generous. Maybe, just maybe this was the answer that she needed.

THIRTY-ONE

TESS RETURNED TO THE COVE, worn out emotionally but at peace. She'd made a decision years ago that hurt people. Perhaps now she could begin to make amends.

She opened the door to the motel room and had never been happier to see anyone.

Vincent rose the moment she walked in. She shut the door behind her and walked straight into his arms, laying her head against the warmth of his chest.

"You okay?" he asked gently.

"I will be. I think." She looked up into his eyes. "Charrie knows her father now; the rest is up to them."

"How did it go?"

She stepped out of his arms and took a seat near the window. Vincent sat on the edge of the table.

Tess told him about Charrie's initial reaction but that she'd finally come down to meet him. "They talked for a long time. I left
them alone." She drew in a breath. "Winston is going to make
an announcement to his staff about his daughter. Neither of us
wanted him to do that. The fallout would definitely hurt his career. But he insisted."

"Brave man."

"A good man."

Vincent was thoughtful for a moment, figuring out how to
phrase his question. "I need to know something," he began.

"What?"

"What are your feelings for Winston?"

"What do you mean?"

"How do you feel about him?"

She glanced away then back at Vincent. "I will always care
about Winston. I won't lie to you. But I'm not in love with him
and haven't been for a very long time. Does that answer your
question?"

"That's all I wanted to know. I don't want us to begin any kind
of life together if your heart is someplace else."

"Winston and I were never meant to be. It was a time in my life
that has passed. We both made choices."

"How much longer do you plan to stay?"

"I need to tie up a few things. It should take only a couple of
days."

"Good. I've been thinking of where we could start over."

"Wait. Before you say anything else, there's something I need to
tell you." She folded her hands on her lap. "I've never told you how
much it has meant to me—all that you've done, all that you've
given up. I know it can't be easy. I don't even know if I deserve it."

He grabbed her hands. "Now, you listen to me. I'm a big boy, and I know what I'm doing and what I want. Sometimes it blows my mind to find myself at this place in my life. But when I think about you, about us, nothing else matters. I don't know what I'll do for a living to support us, but we won't starve, and we won't live on the street. And I'll spend the rest of my life loving you and letting you know how important you are to me. All I ask in return is that you are willing to do the same."

"You get no argument from me."

Vincent grinned. "So where would you like to live—in poverty?"

"I've always loved South Beach."

"Florida?"

"Yeah. Ever been?"

"Nope."

"You'll love it. It's a party town and beautiful."

"Sounds expensive," he said, sounding doubtful.

A slow smile moved across Tess's mouth. "I have plenty of money."

Vincent tossed his head back and laughed. "I never thought I'd live long enough to become a 'kept man.'"

She got up and sat on his lap, turning so that her lips were a breath away from his. "Just think of all the perks." She kissed him long and slow. There was still a part of her that didn't believe she deserved any happiness, but she was damned sure going to suck up as much of it as she possibly could.

Reluctantly she pulled away. "There is just one little thing."

Vincent groaned.

"I need you to do a favor for a friend of mine. . . ."

———

CHARLIE WAS STILL DAZED by everything that had happened. She felt oddly adrift. Even after what she'd tried to do to Tess, Tess had forgiven her. *Her mother.* Although she'd known the truth, having Tess know and accept it made it real. She'd spent so much time hating Tess after discovering her real birth certificate that she didn't know what to do with her feelings now. A part of her still resented what Tess had done. Maybe over time she would forgive her and find a way to have some kind of relationship with her—as her mother.

As for Winston, the hurdle was just as high. They'd both been deprived over the years and were eager to make up for lost time.

Maybe she couldn't forgive Tess, at least not now, but she could open the door for that possibility. Even Mary Magdalene was forgiven.

She reached for the phone and dialed the private number.

"Yes," came the terse greeting.

"I thought you should know that somehow Tess got away. She left sometime during the night. I also thought you should know that I won't be helping you anymore."

Avery listened. A wry smile of defeat formed around his mouth. He didn't bother to respond. He hung up.

What did it all matter now, anyway? he mused. He'd based his whole campaign on nailing her, tying her to those deaths. Stupid on his part. He hadn't banked on Tess McDonald having so many friends.

He hadn't heard from Tracy, and his gut told him that he wouldn't. He clasped his hands behind his head and leaned back in his chair. He'd had a good run. Maybe after the elections were over, he'd take some well-deserved time off, play some golf. He chuckled. And of course there was always private practice.

Avery pointed the remote toward the television to see how badly he was doing in the polls.

TRACY UNLOADED HER VAN and brought the two armloads of supplies and groceries in the house. The doctors said Mark would be released in a week or less, and she was as nervous as a new bride. It had been more than fifteen years since she'd lived with her ex-husband, and she'd never lived with a man since then. As a matter of fact, she rarely let a man spend the night in her bed. Mark had broken down all kinds of barriers, and it really felt good.

She'd gotten a list of things that Mark liked to eat and snack on as well as a pharmacy supply of bandages, antiseptic, ice packs, heating pads—the works. She didn't want to leave anything to chance. She'd even purchased some extra pillows to keep his leg elevated while he watched TV or read.

After she put the groceries away, she went to the linen closet and pulled out all the extra blankets and started putting them in the washing machine. She checked her supply of towels and found that she had enough. Fortunately she had a small half bathroom on the main floor so Mark wouldn't have to worry about going up and down the stairs.

As she worked on rearranging some of the living room furniture, she realized that she was happy, really happy from the inside out. She stood completely still and closed her eyes. The sensation startled her. The feeling was so new and she didn't want to let it go—ever. She was determined to make the best of this, make happiness her priority for once in her life. But in order to do that she was going to have to let go of the past for good.

Tracy went into her study and pulled out the files that Avery sent to her along with all the notes and phone numbers that she'd collected. She brought everything to the living room. She walked over to the fireplace and removed the grate. The flames danced and sparked.

She was so close to uncovering the truth, making the connection, that she could smell it in the air. But some things were best left alone. One by one she tossed every page into the fire. As she watched the flames lick and burn, turn the paper into curling black ashes, she knew that at the center of it all was her sister.

"Wherever you are, Tess, good luck."

She turned away from the fire and continued preparing for Mark's arrival.

THIRTY-TWO

NICOLE PRETTY MUCH had the run of the villa for the past few days. Charrie was off somewhere with her newfound father. Kim was obviously making her own plans, which was fine with her.

She lit a Newport and blew a puff of smoke into the air, just as Kim walked into the room with suitcases in hand.

"I wanted to say good-bye."

Nicole spun around on the stool. "So you're really going, huh?"

"I'm hoping that this will be the opportunity that it seems."

Nicole grinned. "Knowing you, you'll make it what you want it to be, and you'll be running shit in no time."

Kim didn't even flinch at Nicole's language. Maybe she was changing after all.

"We've been through a lot," Kim said.

"Who you telling," Nicole chuckled, but there was a hint of sadness there.

Kim looked down for a moment then into Nicole's eyes. "I made a lot of assumptions about you from the beginning. I wanted to dislike you because of who I thought you were, my own twisted stereotypes. But what I came to realize is that we are more alike than different. We both have our baggage, our wants, our hurts, and our desires. We may have come from different sides of the tracks, but we wound up in the same town."

Nicole was thrown off guard. Her chest tightened. Kim being nice to her, even sentimental. She wasn't sure if she could handle that. This wasn't the woman she knew. But then again, all of them had changed. Even her.

"Thank you for that."

"Have you decided what you're going to do?"

"Sort of. I figured I'd stay here for a while. Tess said the place is paid for through the next few months." She shrugged then looked at Kim.

Kim offered a tight smile. She picked up her suitcases. "Clarke is meeting me at the airport." She hesitated for a moment as if suddenly unsure of herself. "Take care, Nicole."

"I will. You, too."

"Tell Tess good-bye for me."

Nicole watched Kim leave and suddenly felt incredibly sad.

She wasn't sure how long she sat there, but when she actually paid attention again, the sun was setting. She stubbed out another cigarette and looked at the overflowing ashtray. Her pack was empty.

She made for her room. Maybe a nice long soak in the Jacuzzi would make her feel better. When she reached the bottom of the stairs, Charrie walked in the door. She looked happy, Nicole realized.

"Kim is gone," she said simply.

Charrie nodded. "What about you? Are you going to stay?"

"For a while." She leaned against the banister. "You know, I thought some real crazy shit about you." She grinned. "Some of it was true. But I understand your reasons, ya know. Rage is a bitch. It'll make you do things you'd never dreamed of." Her own actions ran like a bad movie in her head.

"I'm tired of being angry," Charrie confessed. "It led me down an ugly path of destruction. I'll have nightmares for the rest of my life about what could have happened. I'm sorry most about involving you and Kim. It was my battle."

"At least you found your folks."

"Yeah. It's going to take a lot of getting used to. I was going to go up to Win—my dad's place for dinner. You have plans?"

"No. I think I'll hang out here."

Charrie nodded. "I'm sorry," she repeated. "I really mean that." She walked away.

Nicole wandered up to her room and stood in front of the bay window. The house was quiet. She could hear the birds outside her window.

In just a month's time, so much had changed. Everyone's lives had been altered. She'd come here with high hopes, the need for something tangible, some roots. Now the very people she thought she'd rely on were leaving one by one, the dream evaporating like water left out in sun.

Tess had Vincent. Kim was set to start over in England. Charrie found her real family. What did she have—nothing but regrets.

Her throat tightened even as tears stung her eyes. This wasn't what she wanted in life. What she'd always wanted was to be able to take care of her family. She'd tried in the only ways she'd known how. And for what? She looked out at the birds flitting from one tree to the next and she cried.

epilogue

TESS READ THE LETTER AGAIN before putting it in the envelope.

Nicole,

I hope this letter reaches you before you leave Aruba. The last time we spoke, we talked about family and about fear. I know that the one thing you want more than anything is to find your sister and brother.

After all that I put you through I wanted a way to make it up to you.

I've enclosed the address for your brother. He's in Philadelphia, just like you thought. It's up to you to decide what you want to do with it. I leave it to you. I know you will make the right choice.

You won't hear from me again. All the best to you.

Tess

She folded the letter, put it in the envelope, and sealed it. It had taken Vincent longer than she'd anticipated to track down Nicole's family. He'd gotten the information only yesterday morning. She put the envelope on the dresser.

Vincent strolled into the bedroom, bare-chested and gorgeous. Tess's heart beat wildly in her chest. She was actually happy and in love with a man who loved her back. Her relationship with Charrie was still shaky, but with time she hoped that it would get better. She hoped to speed the process when Charrie came down to visit next month. As for her sister Tracy, she hoped she was happy and maybe one day they'd see each other again, when it was safe.

"There's an article in the paper about Kim." He handed her the newspaper that was opened to the International section.

There was a smiling picture of Kim next to Clarke. The article extolled the brilliance of their redevelopment plan for several townships in the poorer sections of London. It was a model, the article read, that would certainly be replicated.

"I knew she would land on her feet," Tess said, putting the paper aside. She put her hand on her hip and looked at her husband of three months. "Vince, do you ever regret giving up your career?"

"I think about it sometimes. But with my career, I didn't have a life. My life hinged on the next case." He looked at Tess and grinned. "Naw, I don't miss it."

"Now with Avery out of office, we can always go back to New York."

Vincent arched a brow in question.

"The new DA is an old friend of mine."

"You and your friends." He noticed the letter on the dresser.

"Tess, tell me once and for all, what was the connection between you and Kim and Nicole."

She walked up to her husband and tugged on the waistband of his jeans. She smiled up at him. "Just girl stuff."

That chapter of her life was closed for good, and the events that had bound them would remain secret forever.